SABLE LOCKS AND THE THREE BEARS

Sable Locks and the Three Bears

Dayle House Publishing

Prologue

"Polar. Grizzly. Kodiak. Come on, boys, it's time for breakfast." Mysti calls softly in the quiet of the emerging dawn. Their early morning jaunt down to the shore of the clear, spring-fed mountain lake, with its waters sparkling like fine crystals in the sunlight, is almost a ritual. Mysti stands watching her three fur kids sniff and explore all their favorite spots along the path. The crisp air crackling, Mysti inhales deeply, her lungs feeling as if crystals form on their inner walls. Her nostrils prick with excitement as the breeze speaks softly to the leaf barren tree branches forewarning of the impending lace delivery. Mysti moves like a mist rolling over the forest floor. She halts and hunkers down to inspect a lingering flower now adorned with a dainty headpiece of frost. Standing, Mysti meanders up the path.

Polar, Grizzly and Kodiak walk up beside her, falling into stride. The aroma of freshly brewed coffee wafts down the slope to her from the pot she'd put on the open fire outside her back door. That, too, is part of the morning ritual. Coffee brewed over an open fire had been a part of the fantasy she pictured for many years. Now, she is living that fantasy, at least in part. Mysti reaches the fire pit, bending to remove the steaming brew as the sun inches it's way further above the horizon. She lifts her face easterly, closes her eyes and allows her mind to fill with the ethereal gilded light as she breathes in the rays of sunrise.

Nudged off-balance, Mysti's eyes open. "Polar, that was rude," she admonishes the big white beast jovially. "I know. You want breakfast. Okay, boys, I'm getting it."

After completing the rest of her morning routine, Mysti makes a quick trip into the quaint little town nearby before the roads become too slick and treacherous with the impending forecasted winter storm.

"Morning, Josiah," Mysti greets the burly old mountain man who runs the local Mercantile.

Josiah Westmore is a friendly man hiding behind a gruff bushy-bearded, weathered exterior. "Morning." The single word is grumbled.

Mysti goes about collecting the supplies she needs. She'd heard the weather report and knows that the snowstorms up here can easily be much more severe than predicted and quite often are. With winter arriving, the pantry needs to be fully stocked.

"Everybody musta heard the weather report. Actin' like squirrels, the lot of ya. 'Bout time Y'all started listening to me. Been telling everybody for years. Isn't a meteorologist fella been born yet can predict a snowstorm's intensity better than my bones or my nose," Josiah sputters while tallying up orders and gathering merchandise for town folks. "My bones is tellin' me this un's gonna be a doozy."

Mysti sets an armload of canned goods on a side counter, waiting for Josiah to finish Mrs. Waldeck's transaction. "Would you like me to help you carry your groceries to your car, Mrs. Waldeck?" Mysti offers to the spry, slight built, frosty white-haired woman in her mid-eighties.

"Why that would be wonderful Mysti. You're such a thoughtful young lady it's a wonder some nice young man hasn't snatched you up to take care of him. Lord knows you'd be a wonderful wife," Mrs. Waldeck fusses.

"Ya never let me carry out yer stuff," Josiah gripes.

"Yes, well, Mysti's personality is a bit more companionable, you old coot."

Mysti just smiles pleasantly at the two, long-time contemptuously friendly duo. Shaking her head at the affable banter of the obvious, secretly smitten pair and follows the elderly woman to her immaculate vintage 1950 T-Bird. Her deceased husband had purchased it off the showroom floor. He'd kept it in pristine condition when he was alive. Now that he is gone, her son and grandsons keep it maintained. This is probably its last outing until spring. That is one of the reasons it is in such good shape, it has never been driven in snow and very rarely in the rain.

"Thank you, Dear," Constance Waldeck gives Mysti a hug and advice. "Best get on up to your cabin before this storm hits. And you be sure you have plenty of supplies to last you. Sometimes I worry about you, all alone up there. Then I realize, you remind me of me. Independent and self-sufficient. Drive safely. See you after this one becomes a statistic of history."

"You be safe as well, Mrs. Waldeck. I'd be more worried about you than I am if I didn't know Ol' Josiah is near enough to you, keeping a watchful eye, at the ready should a need arise."

Mrs. Waldeck blushes like a schoolgirl. As she makes her departure with one last wave, the youthful elderly woman sticks her tongue out at Mysti.

Mysti reenters the mercantile, still chuckling softly.

Back inside, Josiah tallies another customer's order and receives payment. Now the only two left in the mercantile, Josiah drops the grumpy front he generally wears.

"How's it going, Mysti?"

"Pretty well, for the most part, Josiah, and you?"

"Side from the aches of a decrepit old man, I can't complain much."

"Yet, you generally do," Mysti teases her elder jokingly, knowing he'd take it well coming from her.

"You sure are a sassy youngin'," They both chuckle companionably. "You mind my word, I'm tellin' true, this storm is gonna be a real hunker down and wait it out, full steam ahead, dumper. Gonna dump more snow in this one storm then a lot of folks see in a lifetime, an' colder than a polar bear's teat. You gonna be alright holed up alone a few days?"

"I fully intend to take full advantage of the peaceful solitude this storm will afford me to work on my book.

"Take care, Josiah. I'll see you when this one, as Mrs. Waldeck put it, is a statistic of history. By the way, I assured her I wouldn't worry about her as I know you'll be keeping a watchful eye and tend to her should the need arise."

This time, it is the burly mountain man who blushes beneath his bushy beard. Surprisingly he reacts with the same gesture as Mrs. Waldeck, sticking out his tongue, causing Mysti to laugh outright.

Sable Locks
&
the Three Bears

by: Remi Dayle

~ 1 ~

Polar nudges Mysti's leg and whimpers. "What's the matter, boy?" Polar whines louder. "You need to go out?" Mysti glances at the clock on the fireplace mantle. It can't be 7:15 already. She's done it again. It feels good too. When she is home in her mountain cabin, it is so relaxing and quiet, time slips by unnoticed. She sits and writes, getting so lost in her stories she forgets all else. Like letting the boys out and eating.

The boys; Polar, Grizzly and Kodiak. Polar is a Siberian Husky/Samoyed cross breed with thick pure white fluffy fur. His piercing blue eyes set in thick black eyeliner and his shiny black nose are his only markings. He weighs only about 90 pounds and is the smallest of her three canine companions. Grizzly is a black and brown, Rottweiler/St. Bernard mix, weighing in at approximately 120 pounds. Kodiak is a unique, seldom heard of breed called the Caucasian Mountain Dog. He weighs in at just under 200 pounds with a long thick fur coat of mottled, deep chocolate brown and black with a smattering of auburn. His head is massive and his build is sturdy. He looks like his namesake the Kodiak bear.

"All right boys. I'm sorry. Time to go out." At hearing the word 'out' all three, race for the back door, prancing and whining with excitement. Mysti opens the door and the boys nearly embed themselves in the doorway as they all attempt to plow through at once. After a few moments of shifting and maneuvering Polar makes it out, followed by Kodiak then Grizzly. It had begun to really snow at some point while Mysti had been entranced in her writing. There was significantly more new snow since her return from town after she and the boys had taken their walk early this morning. "Don't go far!" She calls to the trio shutting the door on the icy wind blowing in. Hearing her stomach growl Mysti decides she'd better fix something to eat as long as she is taking a break.

Dr. Brad Barton looks at his good friend and patient whom he had performed out-patient arthroscopic surgery of his left knee on Friday, just four days ago, to repair the damage caused by a skiing accident. "You need to stay off this leg. Preferably 4 to 6 weeks, but at least a couple weeks."

"I sure wish I could recuperate in seclusion somewhere since I can't go back to work. Maybe I could get some work done on the book I started writing years ago."

"I'll tell you what," Dr. Barton offers "I have that cabin in the mountains. I'll let you stay there for any or all of the next four weeks if you promise you'll sit and write, follow the Physical Therapy exercises I give you and not overdo on this leg."

"Seriously? You've got a deal."

Dr. Barton supplies Dillon with directions and keys to the cabin.

Dillon's brother, Dathan, is acting as Dillon's chauffeur for the day. Dillon tells him of Doc Barton's generous offer.

Dathan drives Dillon home and helps him pack enough clothing for two weeks, food, his laptop and writing materials.

"Are you sure you should make this trip alone?" his brother asks, concerned.

"I'm sure I can handle the drive up. I only need one leg for that, then once I'm there, I will just be sitting at my computer. Are you sure you all can handle the business without me?" Dillon asks jokingly. "You know I'm the glue that holds everything together."

"I'm sure we can handle things for a couple weeks. What about Thanksgiving? You're coming back down, right?"

"Of course."

Early the next morning Dillon sets out on his journey. About an hour into his drive, it begins to snow quite heavily. He muses to himself, *'I should have checked the weather report before I headed out.'* The winds kick up and the snow begins to fall at an outrageous volume. It becomes difficult to even see the road. His cell reception and the GPS are not connecting as he is now deep into the mountains and far from most cell towers. He is unsure of how much further it is to the cabin and at this speed of barely 10 to 15 miles an hour, he can't judge by time. Talking to himself *'Never thought I would need four-wheel-drive. Living in the city having an SUV seems almost silly, but for a trip like this, a four-wheel-drive vehicle would have been a much better option.'*

Suddenly a flash of movement from the side of the road startles Dillon. He swerves to avoid hitting the large animal that sprints across the road before him causing him to lose control and slide off the side of the road, plowing down into the ditch. A few expletives are uttered as he applies the brakes fully, finally coming to a full stop a mere few feet before hitting a tree head-on. He places the vehicle in park. After catching his breath and looking about to assess the situation. Dillon applies the break again and puts the vehicle in reverse attempting to back out the way in which he came. He hears the wheels spinning because there is no traction. He attempts to put it in drive and see if he can maneuver the vehicle forward, to no avail.

"Another fine mess you've gotten yourself into, Ollie." Dillon cautiously opens the door and looks out to see how far from the road he is. However, the snow is coming down at such a rate that visibility is mere feet before him and he can't see the road at all. He determines that he needs to get out of the vehicle and see if he can find a way to put something under the rear tires to gain traction. He grabs his crutches and disembarks the car. The wind is whipping, the snow is blowing, making it nearly impossible for Dillon to maneuver. Realizing he is in no condition to accomplish much, he gets back into his white Dodge Avenger. Dillon checks to see if he has any cell reception to place a call for help. However, his phone shows no service and his GPS doesn't register his location. Dillon sits with the engine running for quite some time trying to determine what might be his best plan of action. He realizes he's not seen another vehicle on the road for quite a distance confirming the road to be a very low use route. As the snow begins to pile deep on the windshield faster than the wipers can keep it off Dillon determines he needs to gather necessary supplies and clothing and head out on foot back in the direction of where he went off the road. He grabs one duffel bag from the rear seat, removes a few clothing items making room to put some water and food supplies. He applies another layer of clothing before donning his winter jacket, scarf and gloves. He writes a note explaining the situation and alerting that he will be on foot attempting to make his way to Dr. Barton's cabin. He supplies the address and the time of his departure then attaches it to the dashboard in case someone comes along and discovers his vehicle. That way they will know who he is, where he is headed and how long he's been out there.

Disembarking the vehicle, he looks around to determine where the road is. Unfortunately, the snowfall rate and whipping winds have obliterated the tracks created on his slide from the road. All Dillon knows is that he was headed up the mountain. He decides to begin trying to make his way in the direction that feels uphill. He places the shoulder strap of the duffel bag across his shoulder and chest, positioning the bag on his back in an attempt to be able to utilize the crutches for support while trying to trudge through near thigh-high snow. He is not making much headway and feels completely disoriented unable to see more than a few feet in front of him, but he keeps trudging on.

Dillon begins cursing himself for the stupidity of thinking this was a good idea. This is how people die in snowstorms. He looks around to see if he can find his way back to his vehicle; however, he has gone too far and can no longer see it or his tracks blown away behind him. Doing his best not to panic Dillon continues trudging in the direction he believes to be further up the mountain, the direction the cabin should be, hoping he will come across some kind of shelter.

He checks his phone for time and service. Still no service. It's now 7:15. He left his car at 5:10. He's been out of his vehicle for nearly two hours.

Exhausted, freezing, disoriented, and nearing panic, just ahead he sees a large tree with a large rock outcropping beneath it and decides to try to get to it. He doesn't quite make it as he stumbles and falls causing excruciating pain in his recently repaired knee. He screams out in agony and frustration. With searing pain and frigid winds swirling around him, his exhaustion begins to overtake his consciousness. He feels a deep desire to just go to sleep.

A voice from within calls to him, *"Fight! Don't give in. You Will Die! Call out for help. Do something, anything. Just do not give up and go to sleep! You'll never wake again."*

Dillon begins yelling into the wind at the absurdity of his predicament. He can't believe these could actually be his final moments of life. He realizes he no longer has pain. In fact, he can't feel his leg at all, nor pretty much any other part of his body. Under normal circumstances, this could have been a fun adventure. However, he is not having fun and is now quite concerned about his chances of survival. *"Keep yelling as long as you can,"* the inner voice encourages.

Mysti watches her three Bears romping joyfully in the snow from the kitchen window as she begins to prepare dinner. Suddenly all three dogs' ears perk and tails rise high in alert mode. Mysti goes to the back door and calls for them to come in.

Polar and Kodiak dart off barking wildly, Grizzly runs to Mysti barking just as alarmingly. "What's the matter, boys? She calls out over the roaring wind, "Polar! Kodiak! Get back here!" Kodiak and Polar continue on their mission barking incessantly as does Grizzly at her feet darting toward her and away, attempting to get her to follow him.

"What's up with you guys?" Mysti knows her dogs well enough to know that there must be something wrong or they would not be acting like this. "Okay Griz, let me get my coat and boots. Hang on." Mysti bundles up and turns off the stove. As she passes through the service porch, she grabs her walking stick, a pack of flares, and two large rechargeable flashlights. She heads out closing the door behind her to follow Grizzly. Just about to depart, she decides to grab the boys' harnesses and the toboggan. Who knows, there may be a wounded animal she'll need to transport.

The wind is whipping wildly, the snow blowing, making conditions a complete whiteout. Grizzly is still bouncing back and forth barking wildly, encouraging Mysti to follow him.

In the distance, Mysti can hear Kodiak and Polar also barking incessantly. Knowing they can't hear her she still calls out, "I'm coming boys, give me a minute," Mysti trudges on following the tracks left by her three Bears. At the edge of the property where it meets the forest, Mysti lights the first flare and mounts it to the fence post, marking the edge of the driveway, then continues after Grizzly.

Lying there in the deep snow with the wind howling, Dillon suddenly hears dogs barking wildly as they come charging headlong at him. Dillon struggles to yell out, "NO! Go away! Go away!" the exertion zapping what little strength he has, his eyes close.

Polar and Kodiak slow their approach as they get closer. They begin to sniff the man.

Through the freezing fog of his brain, Dillon decides that yelling at them might not be the best idea. "Good doggies. Nice doggies," Dillon begins to soothe, barely audible. He feels their hot moist breath upon his face. His eyes open slightly to see two huge furry beasts standing over him that look more like bears than dogs, but he sees they are both wearing collars, so they must belong to someone. Suddenly he has a ray of hope. There must be people nearby.

Kodiak sniffs the man from head to toe then the largest beast lays on top of Dillon. Polar lets out a bark and begins to race back in the direction from which they came.

The beast's warmth begins to seep into Dillon. The dog pants in the man's face with his bad doggie breath, but it too is warm. Dillon realizes the dog's body heat is helping him feel a bit warmer. Still struggling to stay conscious, Dillon begins talking to the dog. "Good dog," he reaches and looks at the tag hanging from the collar for a name. "Kodiak," the dog raises his head in response to his name. "The name fits, that's for sure. That's just about what I thought you were when you came running at me. Well, Kodiak where did your friend go? Do you think you could help me up? Then get me to some kind of shelter?" The dog's warmth and comfort begin to relax Dillon and he drifts momentarily into a dream state.

Polar finds Grizzly and Mysti and the two dogs begin barking frantically again, both rushing back toward where Polar has just come from.

"Okay, I'm coming. This better be worth it guys or I just might forget to feed you tonight," she chuckles to herself knowing she would never do such a thing, but she wants them to know she isn't going to be happy if all this is because they found a rabbit hole up in a log or something equally silly.

Dillon hears barking again, only this time there is a third dog. He forces his eyes open enough to see a light flashing and probing the dark of night and blinding white snow.

The form of an Eskimo styled fur-trimmed parka-clad human emerges from behind the two approaching dogs. Kodiak lets out a loud woof as the three newcomers arrive. Moments later the light shines down at Dillon, keeping the fur-framed face of the human attached, a mystery.

Dillon, still very weak, struggles, but forces himself to speak, trying to sound friendly. "Hi. Awfully sorry to get you out in such weather. If not for your dogs, I'd most likely have died in this spot tonight. My car went off the road and got stuck. I thought I tried to walk the rest of the way, but I fell and I can't seem to get back up due to being in a full leg brace. I'm wondering if you might be able to help me to my feet?"

"Do you always run on at the mouth or only when you're lying in the middle of a blizzard?"

Dillon stares open-mouthed. He hadn't thought for one minute, not even one second, that the person might be female. She probably won't be able to pull him up.

"Up!" Mysti commands and Kodiak levers himself off the man, who suddenly becomes noticeably colder.

"Hand!" She commands the man and puts out her hand to take his.

"I'm sorry. I didn't realize you were a woman. I'm much too heavy for you to pull up."

"Hand! I don't plan to stand here and debate your views of women's strength versus men's and freeze to death. You want help or not?" she bites out at this snow-covered mound of man.

Dillon takes her hand and she gives him her walking stick stuck deep into the snow at his side. "Ready? One, two, three," she pulls and he levers himself with the stick and up he comes. Dillon hollers in pain.

"Look we need to get going before my home flare burns out. It appears you are in no condition to trudge through this blizzard. Good thing I grabbed the toboggan."

Mysti commands Polar and Grizzly to come get harnessed, then hooks the toboggan to them. "Let me help you sit down on here."

"But I need to get..."

"Shut up!" Mysti snaps "Do as you're told! Or would you rather I leave you here?"

"No, but my bag..."

"Kodiak, fetch!" She commands and points at the duffel bag

"But it's so heavy," The man begins to protest as Kodiak picks up the bag and drags it to Mysti, who puts the two handles into Kodiak's jaw and he trots away with it. "Home, boy!" she commands. "Are you coming or staying?"

"Coming, right."

She assists him to sit on the toboggan. She picks up his crutches from where he'd fallen then hands them to him.

Grabbing her walking stick and the lead attached to the toboggan she calls out to Polar and Grizzly, "Home, Boys!" The duo begins to pull. Mysti helps to get things started.

"But...Maybe I'm too heavy for them."

"Stop arguing. Shut up and hang on!" she indicates the rope handles along the edges.

Polar, Grizzly and their human get the toboggan going at a pretty good clip all things considered. Kodiak has charged ahead. His trail leads the way for them to follow.

Dillon's body temperature begins to drop again. He begins to drift in and out. Somewhere in his freezing brain, he notes the sensation of almost floating as he is traversed over the blustery terrain.

Finally, the home flare comes into view through the wind-whipped snow, followed shortly thereafter by the lights from the kitchen window.

Kodiak sits waiting at the door with the duffel bag lying next to him.

"Good boy, Kodiak. Good boy," Mysti calls to him.

Mysti unharnesses the other two dogs before assisting her nearly frozen abominable rescue up from the toboggan and then up the steps. Once on the porch, she opens the door allowing the dogs to proceed in "Fetch Kodiak!" Mysti repeats the command and the dog takes the duffel bag with him. She removes her gloves and hat and praises all three dogs then sends them off to lie down for a well-deserved rest.

The trek had been long and arduous. Mysti now aids the man into the service porch. His breathing is extremely labored, his face fire truck red with bluish-white areas appearing on his cheeks and lips. He is an obvious pain. Mysti removes her outerwear and aids the man out of his also. Hanging gloves and jackets to dry, she notices the rest of the man's clothing is also snow-covered and wet.

"Strip," she commands the stranger.

"Excuse me?" Well, that's one way of shocking his mind awake

"I'll get the coffee started," she states starting to enter the house. Seeing the man has not begun to remove his clothing she repeats "I said strip. I'll start the bath water," with that, she turns and goes to do just that.

Dillon slowly begins removing his clothing, realizing she's right. Everything is wet and cold. He needs to get out of them. Still, he argues, "My leg still has stitches. I can't soak in a tub."

Exasperated Mysti sighs, "Take off your pants. I'll take care of it."

His eyebrows shoot up "My pants?"

"Just do it!" she leaves him to struggle with removing his boots and pants. She returns to find him standing with a towel, he'd picked up from the laundry pile, wrapped around him. She didn't think there was a man alive with such modesty. "Follow me," she commands leading the way to the bathroom.

Dillon notices the box in her hand as he follows her, attempting to use one crutch while holding the towel as securely as possible with one hand.

Once in the bathroom, Mysti turns off the tub taps. "Sit," she commands as she turns to the medicine cabinet and withdraws a roll of adhesive tape. The man looks at her as defiantly as a near-naked man still shivering from nearly freezing to death can, and informs her, "I am not one of your dogs."

"Sheese," she sighs, shaking her head, "I could always drop you back out in the snow and leave you there..." She let the threat hang momentarily. "Please sit down?"

The man complies. "What are you doing?" he questions as she removes his leg brace, then begins to wrap the midsection of his left leg where the four-inch incision runs down the side of his knee.

"My older brother had similar surgery from a football injury years ago. My mom would wrap it in saran wrap and use water-proof adhesive tape for him to shower," Mysti explains as she performs the actions she speaks. "Get into the tub. Add hot water as you need it. It will feel hot at first, but it is quite tepid. As your body warms, the water will feel cool. Warm it gradually. I'll bring hot coffee in shortly, along wi..."

"But... I... I'll be..." He stammers.

Mysti chuckles softly as she leaves the bathroom saying, "I'm sure there's a washcloth or hand towel on the towel bar behind you to cover your private sector."

She latches the door behind her leaving the man to wonder at her seemingly complete lack of interest in him as a man. Not that he thought she should be drooling over him, but a large percent of the female population often seems to do just that.

He eases himself into the seemingly hot water and sits with his eyes closed as the heat gradually seeps through his skin and begins warming his insides. He finds he sees this kind, yet authoritative, stranger behind his eyelids. When she found him, she'd been so bundled against the weather in her Eskimo-style parka with its fur-edged hood hiding her face, wearing knee-high Ugg boots, that he'd been shocked to hear a female voice under it all. He was even more shocked once they arrived here and she'd removed the bulky outerwear revealing a tall, slender Indian princess. Yes, that had been his first impression, although he knows the politically correct term is now Native American. Her skin, such a smooth tawny brown, her hair, rich sable silk flowing down her back to her waist. Her eyes...? The only thing that didn't fit her Native American looks. They were the most shocking, piercing blue. Eyes that seemed they could look into a person's soul. Eyes that were... He suddenly senses a movement. Opening his own eyes to see the eyes he'd just been envisioning, watching him with amusement. Good thing he'd put the towel where he had when he had.

"Your coffee," Mysti offers him the cup.

"I didn't hear you knock," he explains somehow feeling... vulnerable? ...lying here naked with this Princess standing over him.

"I didn't," she informs him.

"Oh."

"I hoped you were relaxing and warming up. It appears you were. I had just begun preparing some dinner before the boys sounded the alert. I brought your duffel bag in so you can dress when you're finished in here. There is a roaring fire in the living room. I'll bring your dinner to you there when it's finished," with that, she leaves once again.

Feeling quite a bit warmer and fearing he'd soon resemble a prune, he attempts to maneuver out of the tub shortly after her departure but finds it more difficult than he imagined it could be. He decides to let the water out and dry himself and the tub, so it isn't so slippery. After a few tries, he finally manages his escape from the porcelain monster's grasp.

He rummages through his duffel bag and discovers dry briefs, socks and jeans, but no shirt. In his rush to grab a few necessities, he'd figured his shirt wouldn't get wet under his jacket just walking and it wouldn't have if he hadn't fallen and gotten snow up under his jacket. Food had seemed more important at the time.

He dons his boxer briefs, jeans and one sock, but finds the bathroom too confining to manage the routine of applying his left sock on his unbendable leg. He hobbles out to the living room, finds a chair near the fire and plops into it just as Mysti enters carrying a tray of food.

Mumbling under his breath, "Brad's going to kill me," he groans as he begins to attempt to put his left sock on with his right foot. He realizes his stupidity at having put the right sock on first as he now can't use the toes of that foot for the task.

Mysti sets the tray on the low table, kneels, takes the sock from his hand and puts it on his foot for him "You don't have..." he begins to protest, but the raised brow look shot at him from those azure eyes halts his speech.

"I didn't *have* to drag you in from the storm either, but I did," she informs him. "Macho egos get left outside. If you'd like to stay with yours, be my guest. Go join it."

"I'm not trying to be macho. I just don't feel right having you waiting on me hand and foot...literally. Geez, I don't even know your name."

Mysti draws in a deep breath realizing he has a point. They are strangers and here she is treating him like one of her brothers. Bossing him around, laughing at his modesty. After all, he isn't one of her brothers. If she took the time to think about it, she should be the one embarrassed by her lack of regard for his state of undress during her earlier visit to the bathroom. She feels her face become warm at the realization of what she's done. Good thing she has her mother's Native American French coloring which doesn't outright blush, instead of her father's ruddy Dutch complexion that blushes at the tickle of a breeze.

"You're absolutely right. I apologize. It's just I'm accustomed to dealing with my two big brothers and fell into treating you like one of them. I'm sorry," she stretches out her hand to him in greeting, "I'm Mysti. The three furry beasts who alerted me and found you are Kodiak, the bear rug that warmed you out there. Polar, the large snowball, who was probably the first to you," the man nods agreement. "...and the one who brought me to you is Grizzly."

The man looks at her, her sable, silken locks of hair falling over her shoulders. A sparkle of amusement twinkles in his eyes and his smile lights his face as much as the glow from the fire does.

Mysti looks at him questioningly, "What?" She asks unable to help from smiling back.

His voice is low and holds some of the amusement shown on his face. He gently reaches to touch the hair lying on Mysti's shoulder. "Sable locks and the three bears."

Mysti unconsciously touches the same swath of her hair, catching the man's twist of the fairytale title and begins to giggle slightly. Then they both laugh out right at the silly play on words.

"Only I don't fit into the story."

"I think this is a combined fairytale. You're a character like Rumpelstiltskin and I am now to guess your name."

She's right he hasn't introduced himself, but the thought of making her guess sounds like fun. "Bet you can't guess my name."

"What do I get if I do?" She joins into the game.

"What do you want?" He asks, one eyebrow twitching upward and a lopsided grin playing at his lips.

"You" Mysti's mind answers silently. *"Where did that thought come from?"* She wonders. Well, although she's been treating him like family, he isn't and while she'd stood in the kitchen preparing dinner, she'd allowed herself to inventory the stranger in her bath.

He isn't as tall as her brothers, but then they aren't tall, they're giants. Though he is a good two to three inches taller than she is, putting him at about 6'2". He is sturdily built. Broad shoulders tapered to the waist and trim, as opposed to Hugh and Harlan's massive structures that are thick of bone and muscle. Whereas Hugh and Harlan were originally of fair complexion, now bronzed from many hours of work in the sun, with light blond hair somehow made whiter by the sun, this man has an olive complexion which also seems sun painted and his thick silky umber brown hair has sun-kissed streaks running through making it look like wood grain. His eyes resemble tiger eye stones.

"Can't you think of anything you want?" He asks smiling, pulling Mysti from her wandering thoughts.

"Actually, no, I can't."

"Tell you what," he offers "if you guess my name, I'll surprise you."

"I don't know," Mysti is hesitant to agree, seeing the gleam in the stranger's eyes. She would do well to remember that he is exactly that. A stranger. Not that she'll worry too much. He is no match for the boys, especially in his present condition.

Sensing her apprehension, he assures "Nothing bad. Maybe..." He pauses, "breakfast in bed or I'll bring in the wood or some such thing."

Breakfast in bed! That reminds her, there is only one bed. When her brothers come up, they sleep right here on the floor or at her parents, a couple miles down the road.

Seeing the strained look cross her face the man asks concerned, "Is something wrong? Was it something I said?"

"Oh, well, no... and yes. Nothing terribly wrong, only slightly and what you said just brought it to mind." She looks up at him. Registering that he's sitting there with no shirt on. Her brows draw together.

"Now what? Your face seems to do a lot of talking, but I don't comprehend what it's saying. If you could just put words to it?"

"Where's your shirt?"

"Oh, you see..." he explains the situation.

Mysti rises "My big brothers have probably left a shirt or two lying around. I'll see what I can find," she disappears through the door, which must lead to a bedroom. Moments later she re-appears with a college sweatshirt. "Hear, this ought to do," she tosses it to him. "Our food is getting cold. It's not much, but it's nutritious."

"When you said big brothers, I didn't realize you were speaking of giant-sized," he holds up the XXXL sweatshirt. "Just how big is this guy?"

Mysti smiles. Most people do consider her brothers extremely large. "I think that's Hugh's, he's the younger and larger of the two. Hugh is 6' 8", Harlan is only 6' 6" and they weigh somewhere around 290 and 320 pounds. They're construction workers. They're very muscular."

He puts on the oversized shirt as she speaks. He notices a smile play on Mysti's lips, "What's so funny?" Sounding like a pride wounded child.

"Nothing...it's just... well... you... you look sort of like a gangly boy wearing his father's clothes," she giggles and stammers."

Looking down at himself then back at Mysti, "Well, that's about what it feels like. Remind me to behave when I meet them. I have a feeling if I did something wrong, they could squash me like a bug!" Then almost to himself finishes again looking down at himself, "And I always considered myself a good-sized man," he looks up at Mysti standing, looking contemplative. "There you go again. Your face is saying something, but I don't understand.

He'd said, *"When I meet them."* When and why was he thinking he would be meeting them? She let that pondering pass.

"When you mentioned breakfast in bed earlier it dawned on me, there is only one bed and two of us."

"You've already been more than helpful. I'll head over to the cabin I'm staying at in just a..."

"Just what cabin are you talking about and how the heck do you intend to get there? In case you hadn't noticed, there is a blizzard raging out there, you don't have your car and you can barely walk."

"Dr. Barton's cabin. It's just..."

"Over 2 miles further up the road. Who do you think you're kidding? I think your brain froze and gave you some kind of amnesia. Did you already forget all that fluffy, cold, white stuff out there that you nearly froze to death in already once today? Do you plan to try again?"

"I don't plan to impose on you any..."

Again, she cuts him off "You don't have an option here. Besides it's not completely your fault and you're not imposing, all that much."

"Geez, thanks. I think," he isn't quite sure how to take that. "OK, I'll sleep on the cou..." He trails off as he looks around the small room.

"As you've just noticed, there is no couch."

"Then I'll sleep on the floor."

"I don't have a sleeping bag. Look..." She goes on before he can attempt any more options. "There's only one bed, but it is king-size. I'm sure that as two mature adults, we can share a bed without any problems. I can," the last two words are stated in such a way that it is a challenge.

Fine, he thinks, she seems totally unaffected by me so it isn't likely she'll start anything and never have I and never would

I force myself on any woman. "Are you always this trusting of strange men whose names you don't even know?" a slight teasing to his tone.

"I've never been in a situation where I needed to consider trusting a man this much, stranger or otherwise, but..." She breathes deeply, "it really isn't a matter of how much I trust you."

"Oh? Why is that?"

"I trust *The Boys.* You try *anything*, they'll have you for a late-night-snack!" Mysti finishes smugly.

He glances around at the three breathing fur rugs, noting their size. "I don't doubt that for a second," he smiles. Then good-naturedly says to the boys, "No offense guys, but there will be no snacks tonight." Again, speaking to Mysti, solemnly, "Rest assured I wouldn't try anything even if they weren't here to protect you."

Strangely, Mysti wonders if that is because of a strong character trait or if he is in some way letting her know he isn't interested in or attracted to her in the least. At that thought, a peculiar feeling of disappointment comes over her, but then why should she care if this strange man finds her and her cabin anything other than a safe haven from a brutal storm? That thought makes her aware of the intense sound of the storm, which she'd all but forgotten. She walks to the shuttered window, opens the shutter and looks out into the blizzardy night. Re-closing the shutter after her appraisal she says, "I'm going out for another load of wood then I'll re-stoke the fire. It's getting late. Eat your food it's getting cold."

He must admit, he is hungry. The plate Mysti prepared for him is piled high with delicious looking rich, creamy homemade mac & cheese with a, was warm, now cool, cornbread muffin on the side. He takes his first bite of the mac and cheese... "Umm! This is delicious. It's smoky with a kick."

"Yes, I use smoked paprika and cayenne in the sauce. Oh, and by the way it's vegan cheese."

"Really? Wow. You better hurry and get in here and eat or I might eat yours too," Dillon chuckles.

Mysti hauls in a couple more loads of wood from the wood-shed out back and re-stokes the fire before sitting down to eat.

A comfortable silence falls between them as they enjoy their meal while listening to the wind bellow and batter the cabin walls. Once finished eating Mysti rises and carries the dirty dishes to the kitchen sink. Dillon's offer to help is declined. Dillon makes his way back to the restroom to collect his duffel bag and carry it into the bedroom.

Mysti stands staring out the window at the irate blizzard. A deep shiver overcomes her as her mind begins to play out the scenario of what would have happened to this stranger had the boys not heard and found him. What if she hadn't listened to them and followed them out in the blustery storm? The hor-rible fate she knew would have been his, causes her to shutter. Shaking her head to dispel the vivid imagery of what could have been, Mysti determines to leave the dirty dishes till morning. She is exhausted. Mysti tidies up the living room and tends the fire once more.

"Side of the bed preference?" Comes the deep voice from inside the room as she closes up everything for the night.

Mysti thinks for a moment. "I would think maybe you should sleep on the far side as it's your left leg injured, that way there is less chance of me bumping it during the night."

"Good thinking." comes the reply. "You coming to bed soon?" He asks.

"Shortly."

A few minutes later Mysti hesitantly enters the bedroom. She finds the man sitting on the far, left side of the bed still clothed. He looks up at her approach, "I thought I'd better wait and let you get ready for bed first," he says rising from the bed. "I'll wait in the other room till you're safely in bed."

Mysti responds simply, "Thank you" as he leaves the room. Mysti strips quickly and redresses in the long-sleeved T-shirt and stretch pants she wears to stay warm on such nights as the fire fades by morning and the inside temperature drops noticeably.

She goes to the bedroom door, "You can come back in now."

As he enters the room, he states "If you have an extra blanket, I thought I would sleep on top of the bed covers fully clothed so you might feel more comfortable."

Mysti looks at the man knowing she could very well be being foolish, but has always gone with her gut instincts and has seldom been wrong and this time her instincts tell her he is no threat.

"Look," she pauses, still not knowing his name, she fills in the blank "Peg Leg, dress for and get into bed. As I said before, I don't need to worry about trusting you," she smiles, whistles, and continues as the three fur rugs come to life and bound into the bedroom to plop again. "I trust my boys with my life," with that, she climbs into bed.

The man smiles back saying, "I generally undress for bed. I don't wear pajamas, is that going to be a problem?"

"Only for you as it tends to get quite cold in here by morning," she answers flippantly as she squeezes her eyes shut tight against the sudden vision of the body she'd seen so much of earlier that evening, lying next to her, in bed. However, try as she might the vision becomes all too clear in her mind and a peculiar warmth, spreads through her. She keeps her eyes closed but hears the rasp of the zipper of his jeans and feels her body tense. She feels the mattress sink and tip under his weight as he sits on the edge to struggle to remove his pants. Finally successful, he pulls off the loaned sweatshirt, maneuvers his injured leg onto the bed under the covers, lays back and sighs. They lay silent a few moments. "Mysti?" He whispers

"Yes?"

"Thank you for...everything. I would literally be frozen to death by now if it weren't for you."

"You're right, you would be. You're welcome."

"Somehow I'll repay you," he says sincerely.

"Don't worry about it."

"Good night, Mysti."

"Good night, Peg Leg Stranger," her final thought as she drifts off to sleep is that he truly is still a stranger. She knows nothing about him, not even his name.

Her dreams are filled with games, guessing games, and baby books of names as she searches page after page trying to find a name that fits the stranger at her side. It would have to be something different. Somehow, she doesn't think he has a common name like Mike, John, or Dave. At some point, she finally stops dreaming. Somewhere in her haze of sleep, she knows she is cold. She huddles deeper into the covers pulling them close around her, finally feeling warmer she sinks deeper into a restful sleep.

Dillon fights for sleep for some time. The realization of how, if not for the furry companions of the beautiful woman beside him, he literally would not have survived this night, would not be alive at this moment. Without a doubt, he owes all four of them his life. How can he ever repay such a debt?

As he begins drifting off to sleep the woman beside him stirs, brushing a hand along the side of his ribs. The sensation evoked by the innocent touch ignites his body and imagination. What would it be like to have those feminine, yet strong, hands trail lazily along his back? To have those command-uttering lips soften and blaze a path of their own across his skin. Stop! He silently commands his wandering thoughts. He concentrates on just going to sleep and at some point, he finally does. Sometime during the night, he realizes he feels quite cold and tries huddling deeper into the covers. Finally feeling warmer he sinks deeper into a restful sleep.

~ 2 ~

Mysti wakes early, as she always does. Why couldn't she just sleep in for once and enjoy the warm comfort of sleep, safely wrapped in strong arms? What? Her mind screams. Suddenly Mysti's eyes fly open. Her body tenses. She tries to recall the events of last night. Remembering, she begins to relax a bit. She told him it would get cold. Like a shivering child, he is pressed up against her. Or is it she who is pressed up against him? She wonders as she realizes she is on his side of the bed. Had she been the one to move to him in her sleep? She doesn't want to think about that.

Get up. That's what she needs to do now, but without waking him and having him find her in this 'too close for comfort' position. Yet, as she inches herself away from the sturdy warmth of his body, her mind taunts how comfortable it is. How nice it would be to stay in this comfort and be able to return night after night. Enough! She commands herself silently. She doesn't want any emotional ties to any man. Besides this man is a stranger she knows nothing about. A situation she plans to remedy right now.

She carefully rolls off the bed checking to see if she disturbed him and finds him still sleeping like a baby. She stares at him a bit longer than she intends, noting how innocent his features look in sleep. A lock of his hair has fallen over his forehead

29

and her hand raises automatically to brush it back, but she catches herself short of following through with the action. She has to reign in her writer's imagination. She is getting carried away with her wandering thoughts just like the characters in her books.

Giving herself a mental shake Mysti takes control once again. She gathers up her warm clothes quickly and quietly to take them to the bathroom to change.

Just before leaving the room, she sees the man's jeans lying there, his wallet protruding from the pocket. Quickly, before her conscience takes over, she removes and opens it. The driver's license picture is not bad, as driver's license pictures go, the name on it is Dillon Marshall Lubbers. "His mother must have been a Gunsmoke fan," she thinks to herself with a smile. A quick glance at the date of birth shows him to be two years older than her own 33 years. In fact, his birthday is January 18th, only two months away.

Her eye catches sight of some business cards in his wallet. She removes one from the stack. It reads:

Land-Lubbers-Scaping

Residential and Commercial New Construction Landscape Specialists

Landscape remodeling and maintenance

3-D.Lubbers@bizmail.com

55-SCAPE / 557-2273

Mysti decides he'll never notice one missing business card from the stack so she'll keep it. She tiptoes out of the room all the way to the bathroom to dress.

When she exits the bathroom, she sees the boys have quietly come out from the bedroom. She lets them out the back door. Seeing the bright blue patches of sky and blanket of sparkling diamonds shimmering in the early morning rays of sunshine, as well as the ominous bank of black snow-laden clouds to the west, she decides to get moving quickly before round two of the storm hits like a title-hungry prizefighter.

Jotting a quick note to let him know where she's going if he wakes and finds her gone, she leaves it on the kitchen bar where he can't miss it. She tells Grizzly to protect. She takes Polar and Kodiak with her, slipping out the back door. She hooks Kodiak and Polar in their harnesses and attaches them to the toboggan then heads in the direction of the road. "Let's find his car," she tells her companions.

It isn't easy locating his vehicle, but they finally do, about three-quarters of a mile down the road. Mysti can see where the man had gone off the road, evidenced by damage to small saplings and bushes. She unpacks all of his supplies and gear from the car and straps it to the toboggan securely before heading back as the sky begins to darken and the snow begins to fall again. Once she reaches the cabin, she unhooks the boys and lets Grizzly out so they can all run and play awhile. Mysti unloads the toboggan and carries the man's belongings into the service porch. Entering through the back door into the kitchen, the smells of coffee, eggs and rosemary sage veggie sausage waft in the air. She finds the stranger standing at the stove leaning on his crutches cooking breakfast.

Hearing her enter, he looks up and inquires, "Hope you don't mind. Figured you'd be cold and hungry."

"No."

He looks surprised "Not cold or not hungry?"

"No, I don't mind. Yes, I'm cold and hungry."

Mysti removes her outerwear after completely unloading the toboggan deciding to leave the stranger's belongings on the porch for the time being. On the service porch, she fills three large bowls with dog food for the boys' breakfast and sets them outside on the stoop. She reenters the kitchen to find the stranger has served up a plate of steaming food.

Mysti sits at the kitchen counter and begins to eat. "Thank you. This is delicious and much needed. I hope you don't mind my getting your keys from your jeans. I wanted to get out there and back before the next wave of the storm. It's about to hit."

"No problem. You should have woken me."

"Why? It's not like you could've gone with me. Figured you deserved to sleep in a bit."

"There are no words to express my appreciation for all you have done for me."

They finish their meal in silence. Working together the duo begins clearing the breakfast dishes and getting them washed along with the dinner dishes from the night before.

The stranger asks conversationally "Have you any guesses as to my name?

Mysti smiles. "Let me think. Is it Obadiah?... Zachariah?... Malachi?" She teases.

"Nope," he chuckles at the bizarre unexpected guesses.

"Let's see... A. Adam? B. Bradley? C. Chadwick? D. Dillon? E. Ethan? F. Finley? ..." she begins listing alphabetically. She sees the man's head tilt and eyebrows shoot up with a surprised questioning look. Mysti pauses noting the look on his face. "Did I guess it?" She asks trying to look innocent.

"Umm-hmm."

"Which one was it? Chadwick?"

"No."

"Um, Ethan?"

"No." His eyes narrow giving her a curious look.

"Was it...hmm what did I say for D? Does it start with a D?"

He nods slowly still eyeing her suspiciously.

"So, it's the one I said that starts with a D?"

"Yes."

"Hmm, darn. What did I say for D?" she pauses for effect. "Oh, Dillon?" She waggles her eyebrows, smiling innocently.

"I think something smells fishy around here. That seemed too easy."

Mysti giggles. "What? You think I cheated? I'm a writer, with a good imagination for different and unusual names," she feigns a hurt look that he would insinuate she had somehow cheated.

"Maybe, but you could have found something in my car with my name on it."

"I didn't," she assures him emphatically. Unable to keep the mischievous smile from her face and the giggle from bubbling out.

He sees the mischievous twinkle in her eyes and her smile and he reaches to grab her saying, "What's so funny?"

She moves away just before he catches hold of her arm. "Nothing," she giggles moving farther from his reach.

Dillon hobbles after her. "Come back here," Dillon chuckles as he tries to catch Mysti.

Mysti goes around the other side of the big chair that faces the fireplace and flanks the large fake fur rug in the middle of the floor.

Dillon at the back of the chair tries to grab her again, but she backs out of his reach.

"What's the matter, Sheriff? Got a bum leg from fallin' off your horse?"

At the narrow-eyed look Dillon gives her she pauses then continues innocently, "Oh, I'm sorry. That's *Marshall* Dillon, not Sheriff."

"Why you..." Dillon tries to quickly maneuver around the chair attempting, yet again, to catch her, however, he isn't quick enough with his leg in this condition.

Mysti sees Dillon wince and catch his balance putting his weight back on his good leg.

"Okay, okay. Truce before you fall and hurt your leg again," she holds up her hands in surrender. "Sit." She tells him.

He throws her a sidelong glance. "I thought we got it clear last night. I'm not one of your dogs you can give commands."

"Sorry. It's just, it looks like you're in pain."

"Yeah. I forgot my present limitations," he begins to sit down and winces again. "Ah, ah, AH! Geeze!" He halts his move to sit and rises to stand again.

"Don't you have any pain medicine?" Mysti asks, concern in her voice.

"Yes, but I don't like taking it."

"In case *you* forgot. I told *you* last night, macho egos aren't welcome in my house. Where are your pills?" She demands, hands on hips showing him she isn't backing down.

Dillon sighs. "In my shaving kit, which is in the large black bag you brought back."

Mysti goes to the service porch where she'd left his things. A look out the back windows reminds her of the foul weather. She realizes she left the boys out. Mysti opens the door and whistles. The snow-covered fur balls blow in with the gust of arctic wind. She closes the door quickly. The boys shake off their frosting and head through the kitchen toward the living room. "Halt!" Mysti commands and the threesome stops just before the living room entrance. "You know better," she reprimands them. "Stay off the carpet until you're dry," Three heads hang low as the trio turn and find spots on the kitchen floor to lay and dry.

Mysti finds the prescription bottle in the bag, takes it to the kitchen where she pours a glass of cold water then takes both to Dillon who has managed to seat himself. "Here," she hands him the pills and water. "When did you have the surgery?"

"Four days ago," Dillon replies.

"*Four* days ago?" Mysti can't believe she heard correctly.

"Yes."

"You mean to tell me you had surgery on your knee then mere days later you just hop in your car and drive..." Mysti pauses "How far did you drive?"

"Oh, only about 150 miles."

"Only? I bet your doctor wouldn't approve."

"Actually, the cabin I'm headed for belongs to my doctor. He loaned it to me."

"You're joking, right?"

Dillon shakes his head no.

"And he knew you were driving up here alone in a snow-storm?"

"Well, the alone part yes, but he didn't know I'd get caught in a storm."

"Whatever! Why did you have to come up here so soon after surgery?"

"To rest, relax and be alone," he smiles.

"Oh, well, it appears you're going to be unable to be alone, but you can rest and relax. There are books over there," Mysti points at the entertainment center, "in the corner by the TV, which you may watch as long as you don't have it too loud, as I have work to do. You know where the food is, help yourself. I brought back all your provisions from your car. I'll get them in from the service porch shortly. You know where the bed is if you feel like taking a nap. I don't want to sound rude, but whereas you came up for R&R, I came up to get some work done."

Dillon watches as she heads for the porch. "What kind of work?"

"I'm a writer," Mysti supplies the answer as she disappears through the porch door. She reenters with the box of food she'd brought from his car.

"Here, let me help you," Dillon offers as he goes to get up from the chair too quickly, "OW! criminy, sakes!" he hollers.

"Sit down!" Mysti orders

"Yeah, yeah, okay."

Mysti goes about unpacking the food and putting it in the cupboards, mumbling to herself as she does "...alone. And just how did he plan to do everything without help? Stupid men, thinking they can do it all... Don't need anyone's help... Well, sometimes they learn their lesson the hard way... Surgery... take off like a wounded dog to lick their wounds...macho bull... proves their pride quotient is higher than their intelligence quotient."

Some of what Mysti is babbling about gets drown out by the noise she is creating accomplishing the task, but Dillon gets the drift of the rambling. Dillon smiles to himself allowing his eyelids to slide closed to rest. Mysti's words begin to fade and his thoughts become fuzzy. The thought that he feels no more pain registers vaguely as he sinks deeper into the comfortable silence of sleep.

Mysti finishes what she is doing and begins to fix herself a fresh cup of coffee. "Would you like another cup of coffee?" She asks then stops to look at the man in the big chair. Noticing the limpness of his body, she realizes he has dozed off. She picks up her cup and walks into the other room. She stands in front of him watching the light from the fading fire dance over his placid face. She takes in the masculine, yet gentle, features. The bronzed slightly weathered skin gives him a rugged outdoorsman look that is softened by the thick lash-fringed eyes, bracketed by laugh lines and the evident creases of dimples. He breathes deeply, sighs and turns his head to one side causing a lock of his long, woodgrain-colored hair to tumble onto his forehead. The urge to gently brush it back comes over her just as it had earlier that morning. Again, she resists. She sighs and moves on to her work corner where she sets down her coffee, turns on her computer, pushes the appropriate buttons to access the story file she will be working on. She then re-stokes the fire before settling down to work.

Dillon begins regaining consciousness. He hears a click, click, clicking sound and slowly opens his eyes slightly and registers that its origin is Mysti typing on the computer. He remains still just watching her through his sleep-hazed, half-open eyes. Her silky sable hair shimmers in the firelight as he watches Mysti arch forward to bring her head back, stretching her back, the movement indicating she's been sitting there quite some time, but just how long? How long has he slept? Dillon realizes he is no longer staring at Mysti's back. While he's been pondering time, she's turned to check on him.

Seeing his half-open eyes, Mysti inquires, "How are you feeling sleepyhead?"

Now it is Dillon's turn to stretch, moaning as he does. "Fine, I think. How long did I sleep?"

Mysti glances at the clock above the fireplace. "About two and a half hours. Long enough for about another six or seven inches of snow to fall," she informs him. She'd checked out the window a while ago only to discover it is still coming down in blankets.

"Two and a half hours!? I told you I don't like taking pain pills. They just wipe me out."

Mysti pushes the appropriate buttons to save the work she's accomplished, stands, stretches and heads for the kitchen. Kodiak notes her direction first and follows. "You want out Kodi?" She asks the breathing fur coat. At the word "out" Kodiak heads for the back door, immediately followed by his instantly awakened brothers. Mysti lets the trio out into the blustering wind, knowing they'll want to romp in the snow a while before wanting back in. Closing the door quickly, shivering, she calls to Dillon, "How about some lunch?"

Dillon carefully levers himself out of the chair as he responds, "Sounds like a good idea. I'll help, considering I planned to be taking care of myself and it's not your job to wait on me. What sounds good?" he asks entering the kitchen.

"I was thinking of having a grilled cheese sandwich, smoked paprika tomato soup and a glass of milk."

"My mouth is watering already," he enthuses. "What can I do to help?"

Mysti begins opening a soup can. She hears Grizzly paw at the door and Polar whine. "Do you think you can manage to get to the door to let the boys in?" Wondering, as she asks, if that is a wise idea. She knows the boys can be a bit rambunctious on reentry.

"No problem," he assures already making his way to the door.

The three bears thunder in, shaking loose the frozen lace. "Mellow!" Mysti commands and they settle, slightly.

Dillon reenters the kitchen closing all doors behind him shivering. "Geeze! It's still a blizzard out there. Can hardly see ten feet. Do you know when they think it's going to stop?"

Mysti hands Dillon a butter knife. She's set the butter dish on the counter next to a loaf of bread. "Here, butter one side of four slices while I go turn on the news."

When TV turns on a special news update about the weather is on.

"This storm was expected, but the intensity was not. Meteorologists say it's never an exact science when predicting the weather. There's always some element of surprise, and boy what a surprise we got this

time. This Arctic blast has brought single-digit and sub-zero tempera-tures with the wind chill factor dropping us into double-digit subzero temperatures. Blowing and drifting have closed many roads as snow-plows struggle to catch up, as keeping up is out of the question. Some have reported traveling friends and relatives missing. They may very well be fine without any way of getting in touch as some phone lines are down and cell signals are even being affected by this massive front. Let's hope that's all it is. George Phelps reporting live from somewhere in the middle of a whiteout blizzard. Back to you in the nice warm studio," the reporter signs off.

"Some areas have already gotten more than two feet of snow since this storm started and with snow still falling and more on the way we could see up to 5 feet in some of the highest mountain elevations before this is over. Stay in and stay warm. Don't go out unless you absolutely must and to those that must, our thoughts and prayers are with you. Be careful." The anchor concludes the report. The automated message concludes the news break, "This has been a CBS special report now back to our regularly scheduled programming."

Mysti has returned to the kitchen counter to continue with food preparations while they listen. They are both silent for a while as they work, each lost in their own thoughts. Dillon is the first to break the silence.

"Do you have a phone here? I don't know where my mind has been. I told my family I'd call when I arrived. I planned to use my cell phone, but it hasn't had a signal," he finishes almost to himself, "I may very well be one of the missing relatives they talked about."

At the mention of family, a peculiar feeling comes over Mysti. Of course, he has a family. Why hasn't she even thought of that before? Family as in mother, father, siblings is probably certain, but she hadn't even given it a thought that he might be married with kids. Why did that possibility cause her chest to constrict and her eyes blur? Mysti doesn't want to even delve into the possible causes of such strange reactions. Putting the tips of her first two fingers to her temples, breathing deeply she begins, "Yes, of course. The landline is over on my desk. I'm sure your family is very worried about you. I don't know why I didn't think to have you call sooner."

Dillon watches Mysti as she speaks. "Mysti?" His voice holds concern, "Are you okay?"

"What? Of course, I'm okay. Why would you ask that? You're the gimp remember?" Mysti brushes the strange feelings aside and tries to put a teasing note in her voice.

"Well, your face seemed to go white, like maybe you weren't feeling well."

Deliberately sounding and acting jokingly sarcastic, Mysti places both hands on her hips, "In case you haven't noticed. I inherited my mother's French Indian dark complexion. I have never looked white and probably won't until I've been dead at least a year or two and all that is left are my white bones," she finishes and turns to complete the preparations of their meal mumbling to herself. "I looked white. Like, I'm sure. Like, I have any reason to even look pale," she huffs. Then noting Dillon is still standing there looking at her she turns to him, "Well? Are you going to call your family or not?"

Dillon catches the slight emphasis she places on the word family and smiles knowingly. "Yes, I'm going to call, but they've waited this long I'm sure they can continue to wait until we finish eating."

"*Men!*" Mysti huffs. She wonders how he could have forgotten to call his family, then when the idea is brought up to him and the fact that they are probably worried, he passes it off saying "they can wait"? She is glad to get this glimpse of his character so she won't be fool enough to become involved with such an uncaring man. Though she pities the woman, who is. A little voice in her head taunts, *yet you envy her too.* Mysti shakes her head to rattle those kinds of thoughts out of forbidden territory. She sets their sandwich plates and soup bowls on the dining counter.

"Are you sure you're alright?" Dillon asks once again. At the sharp look, she throws his way he goes on, "You seem a bit upset since the weather report. Are you nervous? Worried? Or what?"

Realizing she is making a big deal about nothing, and that none of this is any of her business anyway. She draws a deep, steadying breath collecting herself and fabricates the reason for her agitation. "I'm fine. It's just my writer's imagination getting carried away. I just started feeling the desperation of the people stranded and the ones waiting, worrying. Anyway," she finishes lightening her tone, "let's eat."

When they finish eating Mysti begins cleaning up.

"I'll help." Dillon offers.

"No, I'll do this. You make your call."

"You're sure? I feel like you're doing everything. I'm not completely disabled. I can still do some things." Dillon winks.

Mysti chooses to let the innuendo pass "I know you can, that's why I was going to ask you to stoke the fire while you're over there by it. Thanks," Mysti goes about her tasks.

Dillon knows she understood his teasing suggestive tone and wink. He wonders if she is truly unaffected by him. Not that he is conceited and wants her to be, he assures himself. It's just that he… "I what?" He asks himself as he makes his way to the fireplace. He stands staring into the flames wondering why it almost seems to bother him to think he doesn't appeal to her in the least, yet… there was a moment a while ago at the mention of family she seemed upset. At the time, he thought it was because she thought he might already be taken, now the thought strikes him that he knows nothing about this woman. Maybe she has a family. A husband, maybe kids. Maybe that's why she had come here, to get away and get some work done and here he is practically flirting with her.

So many maybes run through his mind. Shaking his head, he pushes them aside. He'll have to try to find out something about her, so he doesn't end up giving himself *foot-in-mouth disease.*

After stoking the fire, Dillon sits at the computer desk and makes his call home.

"Hi, Mom...Yes, I'm fine... Yes, I did have some trouble... No, I'm not at Barton's cabin... That's why I haven't answered the phone... Well, it's a bit of a long story, that's why I'm calling."

Mysti tells herself not to listen in on this conversation, but it is actually impossible not to over hear. The cabin is small after all and Dillon is speaking quite loudly. The first thing that registers is that he begins the conversation with 'Hi, Mom.' Dillon begins explaining how his trip has gone, how he got stuck and the events that followed. Dillon details how Kodiak had played the part of the blanket during the search and rescue and Polar had gone to direct Grizzly and their human companion to his location and so on... "I was saved by Sable Locks and the Three Bears... Yes, Mom. She is a woman and a very beautiful one at that." Dillon shoots Mysti a smile.

His expression changes to humorous disbelief as he listens to his mother. He motions for Mysti to come close and listen. She shakes her head no, but he urges and mouths, "Please."

She does as he requests. Dillon tips the phone so Mysti can listen in.

"Now you behave yourself, young man," the woman's voice comes across the line, "Mind your manners and don't you make her think just because you're injured you need to be waited on and for heaven's sake, no hanky-panky!"

Dillon rolls his eyes. "Aw mom," he whines, a twinkle of mischief in his eyes. "but I'm not a saint and there is only one bed and..." he winks at Mysti.

"Now you listen here," his mother cuts in, "look what happened with Carla. You didn't know enough about her before you let yourself get carried away. You don't know this young lady either..."

"Mom!" Dillon cuts her off.

Mysti steps away feeling this is not a conversation she should be part of.

"Mysti is *nothing* like Carla," he continues. "Yes, her name is Mysti. Mom, don't worry. I was just getting you all worked up. Of course, you make it so easy and fun. Don't worry, as Mysti says, you don't have to trust me, she trusts the Three Bears. If I try anything, she has assured me I'll be a midnight snack for the furry trio of bear rugs."

"Smart lady to have such good protection," his mother states. "May I speak to her for a moment, please?"

Dillon holds out the phone toward Mysti. "Mom wants to talk to you."

"To me?"

Dillon smiles and nods.

Taking the phone in suddenly shaky hands, Mysti clears her throat, "Hello?"

"Yes, hello, Mysti? This is Glenda. Dillon's mother. How are you?" The woman on the phone begins the conversation.

"Fine, thank you and you?" Mysti doesn't know what to say or why she is even talking to this woman.

"I'm better now, much better knowing my son is all right. I hear if it weren't for you and your dogs, Dillon would have frozen to death. Sometimes I wonder if God forgot to give him common sense or a brain for that matter. Anyway, he wouldn't listen to me when I told him going up there was a dumb idea.

"Now, the reason I wanted to speak directly to you is, I want you to know you are not to let him sit around and have you wait on him. He chose to take off alone and not let his family care for him. Said he'd rather do this on his own. Well, as fate has it you got stuck with him, but don't you let him play on your sympathies. Just because he's good-looking and hurt, don't go easy on him."

Mysti smiles as she sees Dillon mouthing words in blah blah blah form imitating his mother.

"And..." His mother continues," if he tries any hanky-panky, you go right ahead and sick those dogs on him. He'll get what he deserves. Now don't get me wrong I love my son and he is a good boy, but I know even the best men thrown into particular situations can lose control and sometimes do what they wouldn't ordinarily do and he did say you're beautiful and I know he wouldn't lie about a thing like that. You take care and keep in touch. It looks like you two are going to be snowed in up there at least a few days. Let me talk to Dillon again, please. Bye for now."

"OK, bye," is all Mysti can think to say and hands the phone back to Dillon.

Dillon ends the conversation while Mysti returns to the kitchen to put on a pot of coffee.

"My love to Dev. Tell Brooke and the other kids I'm fine and give them big hugs from me. Talk to you all soon. Bye, Mom," Dillon hangs up

"Sorry about that. Mom can get a little...?" Dillon apologizes as he comes to stand at the counter "A little intense. I guess that's one way to describe her."

"Well, all mothers have their idiosyncrasies. Would you like me to tell you what she had to say?" Mysti asks while she sets out coffee cups and fixings.

"Let me guess," Dillon begins, changing his voice to imitate his mother's tone. "I told him this trip was a stupid idea, but he wouldn't listen. He wanted to be alone. Now don't be taken in by his good looks and start waiting on him... If he tries any hanky-panky let your dogs have him..." Mysti starts to giggle as he begins his imitation. Now as he finishes, she laughs outright.

"You know her well," Mysti tells him, still laughing.

"I love my mom. She is a great lady, but people have always treated my brother, sister and I as if we are something special and Mom's always afraid it will go to our heads and we'll start taking advantage of others. She likes to keep us humble."

"Why would people...?" Mysti's question is cut short as a particularly strong gust of wind assaults the cabin causing the lights and TV to go off. They are suddenly plunged into dark silence. Neither speaks at first. They sit waiting a moment or two as if half expecting the power to come back on. When it doesn't Mysti says, "Great, just great. If it had just been off due to the connections being blown about, it would be back on by now. Since it's not, it means the power line is down somewhere. Which means it won't be fixed for quite some time."

"You're probably right. A few mountain cabins without power are unlikely to be high on the priority list in a storm like this," Dillon agrees.

In the near complete darkness, they realize the fire is dying down. They speak at the same time,

"I'll go out and get," Mysti begins

"I'll go get," Dillon begins. They both stop.

Mysti begins again, realizing what he'd been about to say, "*I'll go out to get more wood if you can tend the fire,*" she puts up a hand to halt the protest he is about to make. "The snow is too deep for you to even attempt to walk through, Pegleg. Besides if you weren't here, I'd be doing it on my own. I always do," with that, Mysti heads for the door.

Once again noting her direction and intent of going out the boys rise to join her. The four of them go out allowing a blustery blast of cold in as they do. Dillon heads to the fireplace, finding it difficult to maneuver himself low enough to reach the dwindled woodpile beside the hearth. Finally, to save himself from falling to the floor, he sits on Mysti's desk chair, scooches out of it, straight-legged, to the floor, then scooches across the floor positioning himself in reach of the logs and places them in the fire. A little poking, prodding and blowing, like a human bellows, he soon brings the flames to blazing life again.

Dillon asks her on one of her trips in if she has any candles. Mysti tells him where to find them.

Mysti brings numerous stacks of logs in from the woodshed. Most of which she piles in the service porch. By the time she comes in with her final load, even the boys have had enough of the weather and come bounding in along with their Abominable Snow Mistress.

Mysti stops in the service porch and shakes off masses of snow as she removes her outerwear, then hangs it to dry.

"You look near frozen," Dillon states as she comes into the kitchen followed by three soggy furry beasts who proceed to pick drying spots on the kitchen floor.

"I am," she informs him.

"I warmed your coffee. Take it and sit by the fire."

Mysti willingly complies. She sits directly in front of the fire on the floor for a while before moving to the unoccupied chair.

Neither of them has spoken since coming to warm by the fire. They sit listening to the symphonic sounds surrounding them.

Mysti grabs paper and pen from her desk to write down the descriptive narrative of the cacophony enveloping them.

The inhabitants of the old cabin, being plunged into the tumultuous darkness of the raging storm with only the flickering flames of the hearth fire for light and warmth, sit listening to nature's uproarious concert being performed just beyond the cabin's walls. Listening intently, they decipher the various orchestral elements. They hear the rhythm section of the crackling logs, the howling and whistling of the woodwinds underscored by the thunderous pounding of the wind against the cabin much like a concert bass drum and the various bellowing and moanings of cellos and violas of the string section..."

They are each lost in their own thoughts.

"Well," Mysti finally breaks the silence speaking as if to herself, "now what? I can't do my work, can't watch TV, or listen to music, I'm stranded in the middle of a blizzard with a strange man, hours stretching before us and nothing to do except stare at the fire."

Dillon, of course, having heard her musings, grins and supplies, "We could always stare at each other."

Mysti throws Dillon a glance intended to show disbelief that he'd even suggest such a thing, but upon seeing his smile crinkled eyes and deep dimples, the idea seems quite appealing.

The change of expression on Mysti's face doesn't go unnoticed by Dillon who waggles his eyebrows and broadens his smile.

"Your mother told you to behave," she tries to sound reprimanding, but Dillon's expression changes to one of a pouting little boy's and she has to laugh, causing Dillon to smile again.

"Do you play cards?" He asks seriously.

"Not often. Besides I don't have any cards."

"I do. I brought a deck in case I got bored I could play solitaire."

"Since we can't think of anything else to do, I suppose cards it is, but I warn you I don't know how to play very well."

"I didn't say I couldn't think of anything else to do..." Dillon teases his tone seductive.

"Cards sounds just fine," Mysti pointedly informs.

Dillon chuckles, rising to get the deck of cards. At his loud sucked in breath, indicative of a reaction to pain, Mysti glances at her watch. "Time for more pain pills."

"No!" Dillon almost snaps. "I mean I don't want any right now. They put me to sleep and it's too early for bed. I'll take some later," then pausing and once again grinning, "that way you won't have to worry later that I might try any *hanky-panky* as my mom puts it. I'll be sleeping like a baby."

Mysti shakes her head then goes about moving the big chairs closer together in front of the fireplace and puts two small end tables together between the chairs to form a larger surface space.

When Dillon returns with the deck of cards they proceed to play a number of different games over the next couple of hours. Dillon teaches Mysti a few new games. Occasionally they pause to re-stoke the fire, refill coffee, grab chips, etc....

The rest of the afternoon and evening wears on and the storm roars on. The boys join the gathering lying next to them on the floor. They don't talk about much of anything outside of the games they play. Later in the evening, they decide they are tired of playing cards.

"We could play 21 questions," Dillon suggests, "It's fun."

"I don't know. I don't think I know how to play it," Mysti is hesitant.

"I'll teach you. It'll be fun. It will be a good way for us to learn more about each other."

"Oh, all right."

"Okay, you think of something about yourself that I don't know, which is just about anything. For example, something about your family, your work, where you live, your likes, dislikes or you personally. For instance, say you're one of 10 kids or whatever then I ask questions that can be answered yes or no and try to figure out what it is. I can only ask 21 questions to figure it out. You understand?"

"I think so."

"You start. Think of something and I'll ask."

Mysti thinks a minute. "Okay. Ready."

"First question. Is it something about your family?"

"No."

"About you?"

"Yes."

"Is it... Your age?"

"Yes."

"Are you 31?"

"No."

"30?"

"No."

"32?"

"Yes. That was too easy."

"Okay. My turn," Dillon thinks. "Start asking."

"Is it about your family?"

"No."

"About you?"

"Yes."

"Your age?"

"No."

"Where you live?"

"No."

"Where you work?"

"No."

"Is it about your marital status?"

"No."

"Is it how much you weigh?"

"No."

"I don't know."

"You can't give up that easy you only asked seven questions."

"Wouldn't it be easier if we just talked?"

"I suppose."

"I tell you what, how about we agree to answer, say five or ten questions the other one asks. "

"Any question?"

"Within reason," Mysti qualifies.

"You're no fun," Dillon teases.

Mysti goes to her desk and retrieves paper and pencils. "First we'll write down the questions we want to ask, so we won't forget."

That task completed they begin.

"How did you hurt your leg?"

"I was teaching my nine-year-old niece, Brooke, to ski. I was holding her up as we were going down a small hill. I was paying attention to her squeals of delight when I let her go for the first time on her own. I skied off to the side of her without looking closely and hit an unearthed and un-snow-covered tree root. My leg twisted and I did a number of flips and rolls down the hill. The twist caused tears to the ACL and LCL, hence the surgery to repair those, but the landing also fractured the knee cap and tip of the tibia."

"Ouch."

"My turn. "What kind of stories do you write?"

"Well, most people refer to them as romance novels. I prefer to call them adult fairytales. You know, love stories with happily ever after fairytale endings. The stuff of make-believe."

"Why would you say that?"

"Sorry, it's my turn," Mysti bypasses the explanation.

"Fine. What's your question?"

"You mentioned you had a sister. Do you have any other siblings?"

"Yes. Dathan, our sister Devan and I are triplets. We also have twin sisters, three years younger, Kayla and Kiersten."

"Wow!"

"Which is what I was referring to earlier about my mom trying to keep us grounded and humble because people have always treated us as special due to being sets of triplets and twins in one family."

"I can't even imagine how your mother survived raising two sets of multiples, but I guess after having triplets, twins seemed easy."

"Yes, mom always said that twins after triplets was like a single after twins. Much easier and the fact that the twins are both girls, she said raising girls was easier than boys.

"I know you have two giants named Hugh and Harlan that you call brothers," Dillon states jovially, "Do you have any other siblings?"

Mysti chuckles. "Yes, one sister, Autumn. She's 18 months younger than I am."

"Are your brothers older than you?"

"It's my turn, but yes, they are both older. Next question. What do you do for a living?"

"We have a family landscaping business. Land-Lubbers-Scaping. We do residential and commercial landscape design, construction and maintenance."

"Do you make your living as a writer or do you have another job?"

"We have a family business, Van Strien Construction. I often help out on job sites as well as in the office. However, writing is my passion and I do as much of it as I possibly can."

"What's your favorite time of year?"

"I generally like all seasons; however, this blizzard is making me rethink my enjoyment of winter. On the other hand, I guess I should be appreciative of this blizzard for affording me this opportunity to meet such a wonderful person."

"Thank you."

Dillon pauses for a moment thinking to himself, okay here it goes, your chance to ask the one question you really want answered, "Married, significant other?"

Slightly caught off guard Mysti hesitates before responding knowing she has wanted to ask him that question but hasn't had the nerve. Here's her chance to sneak it in. "No. You?"

"Nope."

They both experience a moment of internal relief. Their only outward reaction is they each smile.

Mysti knows this next question is none of her business, but it's been whispering in her thoughts since she'd heard the name during his conversation with his mom. Might as well ask. "Who's Carla?"

Dillon's expression turns somber and he looks away.

Mysti rushes on, "Never mind. That's none of my business. I didn't mean to eavesdrop. I shouldn't have asked."

"No, it's fine. You didn't eavesdrop. I invited you to listen, he gathers his thoughts then continues. "Carla is my ex. It was sort of a whirlwind relationship. Things moved quickly. Four weeks after meeting I thought she could be the one. She seemed to be everything I wanted in a woman right up until I brought her to meet the whole family and discovered her truth."

Mysti is intrigued now. "Which was?"

"She was using me to stalk her ex-fiancé who was then dating my younger sister after he'd broken things off with Carla. He'd found out she was simultaneously engaged to another guy."

"What? Oh, my goodness."

"I ended things immediately, but she didn't go away easily. For a while, she stalked me too."

"Wow. I understand why your mom cautioned you."

"Don't forget, she cautioned you too," his tone teasing.

"That's true. Is there something you're not telling me? Are you dangerous?"

"The only thing about me that's dangerous is my charm," Dillon informs, a glint in his eyes.

"If that's the case, I've nothing to worry about," Mysti responds flippantly.

"Are you saying I'm not charming?" Dillon asks surprised and teasingly hurt.

"Nope."

"Nope, I'm not charming, or Nope you're not saying that?"

Mysti smiles sweetly with no response.

At that moment, Dillon's stomach begins to grumble and growl. They both laugh. Mysti glances at the clock on the wall. "Looks like we got caught up in our games and forgot dinner. It's getting late. What would you like to eat?"

"Just something quick and easy. A sandwich?"

"Ooo, yeah. I know what kind of sandwich I want. I was craving one the other day, but didn't get around to making it," Mysti's face lights up at the thought.

"What kind is that?"

"PBDP," at his quizzical expression Mysti supplies, "Peanut Butter and Dill Pickle. Yum," Mysti licks her lips in appreciative anticipation.

"*What?* Did I hear you correctly? Peanut Butter and Dill pickle sandwiches? Are you kidding me?"

"Yes, that's what I said. No, I'm not kidding. They are the best sandwiches. Delicious."

"I thought only pregnant women craved that kind of crazy concoction," Dillon responds in near horrified disbelief that she is serious.

"You don't know what you're missing," Mysti hops up and heads toward the kitchen. "What kind of sandwich do you want Peg Leg?" she teases. "I thought pirates were adventurous."

"Yeah, well, there's adventure and there's risky. I like to play it safe. I'll stick to PB& J."

"That's not true," She retorts. "You took the risk to drive into the mountains alone mere days after surgery. You took the risk to venture out of your vehicle in a blizzard after becoming stranded. Those are so much riskier than trying a PBDP."

"You're right," he ponders her observation before caving in. "Oh, all right. I'll give it a try. The worst that can happen is I don't like it and I have to make something else to eat."

Mysti smiles. "Ah, the wonders of peer pressure," she teases as she prepares a second PBDP.

They resume their seats in front of the fire they've kept continually stoked for heat and light.

"Ok. Here I go," Dillon looks skeptically at the sandwich, then at Mysti to see if she is truly going to eat hers or if this is some kind of joke to see if he would actually eat this. He raises the sandwich to his mouth, then pauses looking over it at her again.

Mysti realizes he is waiting to see if she is really going to consume this strange concoction. "Oh, whatever," she says as she picks up her sandwich and takes a large juicy bite from it, once again licking her lips in appreciation. Chewing enjoyably, she mumbles through her mouth full of food, "So delicious. If you're too chicken to eat it, that's fine."

"Chicken, huh?" With that, he opens his mouth wide, closes his eyes and takes a big bite. After a few chews, he opens his eyes, looks directly at Mysti stating sincerely, "Wow, never thought I would say this but, it is very tasty. Never in my wildest imagination would I have put this together as a combination, but it's good. Whatever made you come up with this?"

"My mom used to feed this to us when we were kids."

They finish off their sandwiches and chips in companionable silence. Their hunger sated they yawn in unison. "It's not like we've done much all day. However, I feel sleepy. I think I'm going to turn in for the night.

"I know. I think I will too," Dillon agrees.

As Mysti rises to let the boys out, Dillon asks, May I use the restroom first and get out of your way quickly.

"That's fine."

After letting the boys out, Mysti gathers her sleepwear, lets the boys back in then takes her turn in the bathroom while Dillon stokes the fire on his way to the bedroom.

Dillon is already situated on his side of the bed when Mysti and the boys enter a short while later. The boys all plop on the floor and Mysti quickly climbs under the covers with a shiver.

"Cold?" Dillon inquires.

"Just chilled. After taking a quick hot shower the house feels chilly," she informs.

"Give me your feet."

"What? No, that's ok."

"Give-me-your-feet," he states emphatically. "Don't act like I just told you to strip like you did me..." he reminds her of her command two days ago.

Mysti realizes he's right. She lays on her side, back to him, and bends her legs bringing her feet up behind herself near his hands. Lying behind her, Dillon, envelopes her feet in his large warm, surprisingly soft hands and begins massaging her feet.

At first, she tenses, but then relaxes into the wonderful sensation and tingling warmth that emanates throughout her. At the moment, she is unsure if the tingling is purely from warming or her body's chemical reaction to the mere touch of this handsome stranger with whom she is sharing her bed. She tries to convince herself it is the first reason only.

"Feel better?" the deep voice asks softly.

Feel better? Those two simple words sounded excitingly husky. It must just be the way his voice sounds when he is sleepy or, simply the way her mind is perceiving it because she is sleepy.

Mysti inhales deeply and sighs, "Much," is all she seems able to utter from her suddenly dry mouth. She stretches out her legs moving her feet back to the end of the bed and tries to settle into a comfortable position still on her side. Dillon scooches closer, draping an arm over Mysti's mid-section. Mysti gasps softly, her breath catching. *"What does he think he's doing?"* her mind demands silently.

"Conserving and sharing body heat," he responds as if reading her mind, "nothing more."

Mysti realizes her romance writer's imagination is meandering into unnecessary territory. Just because she secretly finds him attractive doesn't mean he views her as anything other than a co-human with whom he has had the misfortune of becoming snowbound.

She draws a deep calming breath, exhaling slowly, consciously forcing herself to relax, reigning in her wayward thoughts and settling close to Dillon. She will have to control her wandering mind and be as unaffected by him as he seems to be by her.

As she drifts off to sleep, she realizes that just yesterday, she viewed and treated him as she did her brothers, and he seemed affected by her femaleness. Now? The tables seem to have turned.

As he drifts off to sleep, Dillon hopes he is able to maintain this façade of being unaffected by this beautiful woman. He doesn't want their predicament to become uneasy. He surely doesn't want her to be apprehensive of his nearness. It annoys him that he's bothered that she doesn't seem at all attracted to him because he finds her extremely so. Then again it is probably better this way. After all, once they are able to leave this snow-induced seclusion, they'll probably never see each other again so what would be the sense in complicating matters with unnecessary emotional baggage?

Dillon hears and feels Mysti sigh and relax, evoking a smile as he too succumbs to slumber.

~ 3 ~

The twinkle of sunlight through the slats of the shuttered windows tickles both Mysti and Dillon awake, yet neither moves for a long while, both seemingly content and unwilling to break out of the cocoon of warm comfort they are enveloped within.

After nearly fifteen minutes, "Good morning sleepy head," comes the deep rumble of Dillon's morning voice made husky with remnants of sleep. So near is he, to Mysti's ear that his moist breath tickles her neck causing her to shiver. "Cold?"

"No, you're breathing on my neck and it tickles," she responds honestly.

"Oh? So, you're ticklish, are you?" as he asks he begins tickling Mysti's ribs causing her to giggle and squirm.

"Stop. Please. Don't," Mysti manages through the gurgles and giggles.

Dillon does as she requests, deciding that to continue could become dangerous, with her body squirming against him like that.

The boys waken, helpfully interrupting by making known their need to go out, causing Mysti to maneuver out of bed quickly and depart the room, leaving Dillon to lever himself out of the moments before warm nest.

Mysti brings in more loads of wood while Dillon puts on coffee and starts breakfast. She joins him in the kitchen. "You made a big stink about me calling my family yesterday to let them know I was ok, but you didn't call yours."

"My family knows where I am. I come here often. They aren't worried."

"Even with this storm, they won't be concerned?"

"They know I can take care of myself."

"Still, I think you should check in."

Mysti shakes her head then goes to the phone. No dial tone. "The line is down. The storm has let up. I'm going out to get the generator running."

"You have a generator? Why didn't you start it yesterday when the power went out?"

"Um, in case you hadn't noticed there was this little issue of a blinding, raging blizzard yesterday. I could barely see my own hand out there yesterday let alone access, uncover and start up a propane generator."

"Sorry. That was dumb of me to ask. I know nothing about generators. I guess I somehow thought all you had to do was flip a switch or something."

"Nope, not quite that simple, but I'll get it going in few minutes,"

Mysti dons her outerwear again and gets to it.

Dillon cleans up from their morning meal. A mere fifteen minutes later the TV blares to life startling Dillon. The lights flash, shortly followed by Mysti and the bears entering the service porch, stomping and shaking off their freshly acquired frosting.

"Better?" she asks, entering the main area of the house.

"Success."

The weather reporter comes on with a live update.

"The powerful blasts from this two-punch storm front is finally over. We now move into recovery mode. Snow removal will be targeted

first and foremost on the main thoroughfares and highways. However, some private sector plow companies are offering to begin work on some of the outlying roads where it is believed some motorists might have become stranded and may be in dire straits. There have already been three confirmed deaths from this storm and there are fears the death toll could rise...."

Hearing those words hits Dillon with the extreme realization of just how close he had come to being part of that statistic. The overwhelming intensity of emotion that suddenly consumes him causes his breath to catch and his heart to skip a beat. Without hesitation he steps to Mysti and envelopes her in his arms, hugging her sincerely.

Caught off guard by Dillon's action, Mysti stands dumbfounded arms hanging at her sides. She hears Dillon sniffle just before he lets loose of her and steps away saying, "Sorry. I...it's just... hearing that reporter talk about the death toll from this storm struck me. You *literally* saved my life! I would have eventually been added to that death toll statistic if not for you and your three *bears*."

Mysti hears the emotion choking his voice. Going to him she lays a hand on his arm. Dillon looks into Mysti's eyes.

Mysti sees tears pooling at the brims of his tiger-eye-colored eyes.

"Be thankful for what did happen, but try not to dwell on what didn't. I understand how you feel. I struggle to keep the images of the *what-could-haves* and *what-ifs* at bay. I am truly grateful the boys heard you and that I followed them," Mysti inhales deeply. Shaking off the dark mood, she steps away quickly saying a bit louder, "I don't know about you, but now that we have power I have work to do."

Dillon recognizes her attempt to lighten the mood and follows suit.

"Good idea."

Giving himself a mental shake Dillon goes to gather his laptop and writing supplies from his luggage.

It's not long before the duo gets situated and both set about working on their respective books. The room is filled with glorious sunshine that glistens like fields of sparkling diamonds outside the windows. The trees appear to be coated with pristine white frosting that have been covered with an abundance of crystallized sugar. The azure sky, now cloudless.

The day passes in companionable quiet save for the clicking sounds of two computer keyboards. They occasionally pause for snacks, lunch, fire stoking and to let the three bears out to play.

Deeply engrossed in their inspiration, time seems to both pass quickly, yet simultaneously stand still. All-in-all it is a very productive day for them both.

"Eight o'clock?" Mysti observes. "I'll start dinner," she states as she saves her work and shuts down her laptop for the night.

Dillon saves his work also. "I'll help," as he rises the three bear rugs come to life and without hesitation, Dillon hobbles to let them out.

Mysti smiles as she makes her way to the kitchen to determine what to make. "Thank you for letting them out."

Mysti knows it's not a big deal, but it felt somehow strange, yet nice, to have someone else do an everyday menial task. She is unaccustomed to having anyone do anything for her.

Dillon notices the soft smile and quizzical tilt of her head. "What?"

"Nothing."

"You're smiling."

"Is there something wrong with me smiling?"

"No, you have a beautiful smile. I like it."

Mysti's face flushes warm and she is once again grateful her complexion doesn't allow visible blushing.

"I was thinking of making sautéed party peppers, sweet onion with pan-seared micropeotien-chick-less pieces over Angel Hair pasta, topped with homemade vegan roasted garlic parmesan sauce, vegan mozzarella, and black olives."

"Wow, that sounds delicious. My mouth is watering already. What can I do to help?"

"You can get the pot of water boiling for the pasta while I cut up the veggies."

Once Dillon has the water heating on the stove, he picks up a knife, stands next to Mysti and begins to help cut veggies. Dillon graces Mysti with a sidelong smiling glance and a shoulder nudge, evoking a return of the same.

Dillon lets the boys in, then fills their food bowls in the service porch before stoking the fire while Mysti completes meal preparations.

Sitting by the fire with their meal, Mysti chances a glance to see Dillon's reaction to the food.

With his first bite, his eyes close momentarily with appreciation. Talking with food in his mouth, "Wow. This is good. It's so creamy and...delicious," he drools, nearly spilling food from his mouth.

Mysti chuckles softly. "After having spoken to your mother, I can say with near certainty you were taught not to talk with your mouth full."

They share a chuckle. "You're right. She'd be appalled by my poor manners, but this is so good. Speaking of mothers, I think you should check the phone line and call your family to let them know you're ok."

"I suppose you're right. I will as soon as I finish eating."

Mysti picks up and turns on the cordless landline phone, hearing a dial tone she dials her mom's number.

Dillon takes the dishes to the kitchen area to begin cleaning up.

As was the case for Mysti when he'd made his call, it is nearly impossible not to overhear the conversation.

"Hey, Mom...Yes, I'm fine...Of course, the boys are loving it...We were without power until it let up enough that I could go out and get the generator powered up..."

In the kitchen, Kodiak walks behind Dillon bumping him off balance. "Hey, you big furball, watch where you're going," Dillon reprimands teasingly.

Mysti's mother, Cora, hears the male voice, "Um, excuse me Dear, unless your dogs have suddenly gained the ability to talk, who was that I just heard? Is there something you're not telling me?"

Mysti draws a deep breath before beginning the explanation. "That is Dillon..." She imparts the events of the past few days.

"Oh, my!" Cora responds often throughout the retelling.

"So, we are stuck here together for the foreseeable future until the roads are cleared enough to..." she pauses, "I'm not even sure what the next step will be. Dillon's car will have to be dug out and pulled back up to the road. We're unsure if it has damage that will prevent it from being driven and if so, it will have to be towed down the mountain. Who knows how long it will take before they even get a plow up this far to clear the road? Fortunately, I had stocked up on food before the storm and he brought some supplies, which the boys and I retrieved from his vehicle the first morning. We won't starve and there's still plenty of wood in the shed so we won't freeze either."

"Has he been in contact with his family?"

"Yes, he got in touch with his mother before the phones and power went out. I'm going to have him check in again when we finish talking."

"I am so proud of you and very thankful you and the boys were able to rescue Dillon. I truly hope you are able to get down the mountain by Thanksgiving as I'm sure he and his family will be joy and gratitude filled for his life and safe return. Please give Dillon a hug from me with my heartfelt joy for his survival."

"I'll tell him."

"Don't just tell him. You know better. I'm serious, you must give him the hug to ensure the truest energetic passing on of my sincerity."

"Yes, Mom. I know. I'll give him your hug."

Mysti looks at Dillon to see his reaction to those words as she knows he has overheard her side of the entire conversation.

Dillon offers Mysti an eyebrow wiggling smile to which Mysti responds by sticking out the tip of her tongue before chuckling ever so softly.

"What's funny, Dear?" Cora asks sensing the behind-the-scenes humor taking place. She knows her daughter oh so well.

"Nothing."

"Is he at least easy on the eyes?" Cora asks with a hint of amusement.

"Don't go there, Mom."

"Go where Dear?" Cora now outright chuckles. "Be careful. I know you always are, sometimes too much so, and I know the boys will protect you if the need arises. However, maybe don't be as closed off as you have been. I love you."

"Love you too, Mom," Mysti finishes up their conversation with the promise to keep Cora posted and the hope of being together for the upcoming holiday.

"I heard your mom laughing. Where was she going that was so funny?"

"She wasn't *going* anywhere. She asked a question that alluded to a direction of conversation I have no intention to entertain," Mysti attempts to quash the subject.

Dillon seems to have no such intention. "What direction of conversation is that?" he asks with the same hint of humor her mother had used.

"Fine, she asked if you're good-looking," Mysti hopes that will satisfy him and they can move on. No such luck.

"Am I?" he asks hobbling closer to her, sporting a devilish grin.

Mysti finds herself feeling slightly giddy and flushing once more, almost enjoying the hint of flirtation. She also finds herself nearly 'trapped' in the corner of the kitchen with the only escape route barred by the charmingly attractive stranger.

Dillon moves closer, his smile increasingly broadening with each hobbled step until he is mere inches from Mysti.

Mysti quashes her urge to throw caution to the wind and see what his intentions are in the moment. With her mouth breaking into a broad smile of its own she emits a loud clicking sound. Three bear rugs jump to attention and approach their mistress, pausing behind Dillon, awaiting further command.

Dillon senses the sudden close proximity of all three protectors. He remembers he is still a stranger while also realizing just how very well-trained they are. Dillon cautiously takes one step back from Mysti, whose smile deepens.

"As I have said repeatedly, I always trust my boys," she winks. She then clears Dillon's retreat by stating, "Away," resulting in but a moment's hesitation and three final glares to remind this man that although they like him, their loyalties forever remain with their mistress.

Dillon hobbles toward the living room. Mysti approaches laying a hand on his forearm to halt him. "I promised my mother," she states before slipping her arms between the crutches and his body to wrap her arms around him. "This is a hug from her with her heartfelt joy for your survival."

Dillon grasps his crutches with his armpits and hugs her back. "That's my return hug to her in gratitude for birthing and raising the wonderful daughter who saved my life."

Mysti lets loose, stepping away before becoming caught up in the emotions welling up in her. "She also commanded that I have you check in with your family again."

"Good idea," Dillon sits to call his mother. "Hi, Mom...Mysti got the generator up and running this morning.... Yes, the power went out after we talked and the phones were out too...The phone came back on just a while ago. Mysti called her mom to let her know what's up... Her mom made her promise to give me a hug from her and make me check in with you again...Yes, she gave me the hug from her mother...Mom!... I don't know... hang on..." Dillon turns to Mysti, "My mother would like to know your mother's name and phone number."

"Why?"

"She said 'just in case'."

"I suppose she's right. Cora Van Strien, 555-1828"

"Thanks," Dillon repeats the information to his mom. They chat a few minutes longer, "Yes, I'm still behaving...I witnessed exactly how well trained and protective the three bears are with just the click of her tongue," he tells his mother about the playful incident.

"Be careful and respectful. I don't want you to have survived nearly freezing to death to end up being a snack for your furry rescuers for bad behavior," Glenda jokes.

"Ha-ha. Very funny. I'll let you know if we figure a way out of here. Love you too."

Mysti and Dillon relax and watch a movie to end their day before retiring to bed for the night.

They usher in their Friday morning falling into a comfortable pattern of Mysti tending to wood replenishment, tending the fire, letting out, playing with and feeding the boys.

Dillon tends to making coffee and starting breakfast. He looks out the kitchen window, watching Mysti romp in the thigh-deep snow. He wishes he could join the playfulness. Taking in more fully the surroundings he sees a barn off to the left and across what is probably a driveway area under the mounds of snow. Beyond that, frothy white snow-covered trees. While the coffee perks and Mysti is outside, Dillon takes this time to walk around inside the cabin opening the wooden shutters and taking in the various views. Opening the floor to ceiling shutters along the back wall he discovers a sliding glass door to a covered porch overlooking a lake down a sloped path. Dillon can imagine how beautiful this view must be in other seasons. He recloses the shutters as he hears Mysti emerge on the service porch with Kodiak, Polar and Grizzly. He turns and watches as they appear as variations of abominable snow beasts causing Dillon to laugh outright as they all shake off the layers of snow.

"Do you think maybe the four of you could leave some of the snow *outside*?"

"What fun is that?" Mysti inquires with amusement.

"Breakfast is ready."

"Smells great."

While eating crispy veggie bacon, free-range eggs and toast at the kitchen counter, they discuss a plan for their day.

"I was wondering if you might be willing to take a look at what I wrote yesterday and give me some professional feedback."

"Sure. We could do a book swap. At least do line editing for each other as well as maybe some constructive input."

"Sounds great."

Yesterday when Dillon set to writing he set aside his previous work and began a new project. Dillon's current story is a somewhat romantic mythical fantasy version of a story lightly based on their current experience and situation.

"I usually write light 'who dun it' mystery, but this just poured out of me yesterday. I guess partially why I wanted to have you read it to see what you think is because this isn't my normal genre."

Dillon is apprehensive of her response, but hands over his laptop with the document ready for reading.

Mysti is a clean, wholesome romance writer, working on a book which she is nearing completion of the first rough draft.

They spend their day pouring over each other's work. Pausing for the usual breaks as well as occasional short discussions about one thing or another in the other's manuscript for clarification or praise of content or manner written.

The day again concludes with the joint preparation of dinner followed by a movie. However, tonight, before heading off to the cocoon of the singular bed, Dillon enlists Mysti's help waterproofing his leg for a quick shower. This night, just as each prior night, they find themselves lying close to share and conserving body heat.

For the next three days, after completion of their now, morning routine, they spend most of their time making corrections and tweaking their own stories with plot suggestions and story ideas from each other. They continue with new content which they again line edit for one another.

Mysti finds herself casting what she hopes are covert glances Dillon's way throughout each day. She is surprised at how comfortably companionable they seem. She wonders if that is merely due to the fact they've been thrust into this somewhat intimate secluded situation without choice. Mysti muses to herself that having their writing as a common interest is probably their biggest saving grace. Something in common that gives them the means to escape to their own space, so to speak.

Dillon allows his budding attraction toward Mysti to fuel his writing and the attraction between his characters. His writing has never flowed so freely and effortlessly. At least when he's not covertly gazing at Mysti. He hopes his glances go unnoticed. He's mostly successful. However, at this moment he finds their eyes locked as they catch each other looking. Neither seems to want to be the first to look away.

Dillon's lips slowly curve into a playful smirk.

Mysti decides to break the momentary tension by making a silly, thumbs to ears, fingers wiggling and tongue stuck out playful face, catching Dillon of guard causing him to all out, belly laugh. A rich, resonant sound Mysti finds comforting and attractive at once, causing her to look away first in hopes her emotions aren't evident in her expression.

"Yes!" Dillon cheers with a small fist pump, "I win."

"Yes, what? Win what?"

"I won the stare-down. I made you look away first."

"I only looked away because my eyes are dry and tired from looking at the computer screen all day," Mysti rises to let the dogs out.

After dinner is made, eaten and cleaned up, they plop in the chairs near the fire in comfortable silence.

Monday evening the phone rings startling them both. "Want to place guesses who that might be before you answer? Your mom or mine?"

Mysti chuckles, thinking he's most probably correct. "Hello," she answers, laughter still in her tone.

"Hi, sweetheart. You sound happy to hear from me."

Mysti's expression turns instantly angry; her blood goes stone cold before raging to boiling fury.

Dillon sees and feels the immediate change in Mysti and becomes concerned. Something raises his hackles.

It's obvious Mysti doesn't want to be talking to whoever is on the phone. Mysti looks at Dillon, her expression a myriad of emotions. He sees a touch of fear, red-hot anger directed at the caller and a dose of "I'm sorry' shot toward him.

She holds the phone slightly away from her ear and Dillon leans closer to hear.

"I am Not your sweetheart. I am Not happy to hear from you. What do you think you are doing calling me and how did you know where to call?" she asks, seething.

"Ah, Darling, I was concerned about you. I called to see if you're alright. I saw Autumn and her friend at a restaurant yesterday and heard her saying you went to the cabin to write. I got to thinking about you stranded in that horrible storm, all alone, and wanted to check to see how you're doing."

"How I am is not your concern. You have no business contacting me."

"And yet you answered. You must have wanted to talk to me."

"No, you idiot, I didn't look at the caller ID before answering as I mistakenly gave you credit for being smart enough to never contact me again."

"You know you love me as much as I love you," Dillon hears the voice on the line, coo.

"James, I'd tell you where to go, but even Satan wouldn't let you in. You make him look appealing."

Dillon can't help the soft chuckle that escapes. The caller hears it.

"Who's with you?"

"None of your business!"

Mysti ends the call. And turns off the ringer. She knows he'll call back and she doesn't want to hear it ring. She'll let it go to voicemail.

Dillon looks at Mysti, and seeing her visibly shaking, without hesitation takes her in his arms and silently holds her. A few minutes pass before Mysti inhales deeply, effectively diminishing the shaking and she moves out of Dillon's embrace. "Thank you."

"No problem. Are you OK?"

"I will be. Sorry about that."

"You have nothing to be sorry about. Dare I ask who that was?"

"It's a long story," Mysti sighs.

"Well, last I checked we pretty much have nothing but time for a while still, so..."

Mysti laughs softly, "You have a point."

Dillon decides, this calls for comfort food. What better than hot chocolate and popcorn? They set about making their snack.

Dillon brings over the bowl of popcorn. Mysti carries the cocoa.

"So, who is this, James?"

Mysti fills him in on the lengthy story of an unstable man who merely saw her somewhere... "He developed an unhealthy fixation on me and began stalking me. It became more than just a nuisance. He'd show up places where I was and create scenes demanding I 'come home' with him.

"Wow! I'm sorry."

"He's been quiet for the past few weeks. Now this call. I need to call my sister to let her know that he's probably stalking her to get info on me."

"Good idea. You call her, I'll let the boys out, stoke the fire and get things set for the night."

Mysti calls Autumn and tells her about the call.

"Mom told us about your rescue. How's that going?"

Mysti looks at the man hobbling around on crutches tending to the tasks at hand and a smile creeps into her voice which doesn't escape her sister. "He's a really nice guy. I'm just very glad the boys and I were here and able to save him."

"Mom and I were wondering... What's he like? Is he good-looking? Any Sparks?

"He's an injured man I pulled out of the snow so he wouldn't die."

"Yes, I know that and I am so proud of you, but you didn't answer my questions. Are you saying he hasn't tried *anything*? Not even any flirting?"

Mysti sighs knowing her sister is going to keep nagging her, "Kind. Yes. Sort of. No. A little." Mysti ticks off the answers in the order asked.

"Sort of sparks? A little flirting?" Autumn's interest is peaked.

Mysti tells Autumn about the incident in the kitchen after her call with their mom and how with one click the boys made their presence known. "I assured him I didn't need to trust him as I trust Kodi, Griz and Polar," the sisters share a knowing laugh

Autumn then sobers. "Sis?"

"Yes?"

"If he really is a nice guy, don't put up too many blocks. It's time you let your guard down a little. Not every guy is like James and chances of a repeat of what happened with Jeff are minuscule."

Mysti is silent and Autumn continues. "I know James scares you, but he's one in ten million. And Jeff? I know you still miss him, but it's been 4 years, he'd want you to be happy again, to live life more fully in remembrance of him. He'd want you to remember, you still have a life, don't waste it. Time for you to find love again."

Mysti once again looks at her guest. Smiling, she whispers, "I hear you, sis. I'll try not to put up too many walls, or at least only ones with doors in them."

"Good idea. Then if this guy or maybe someone else finds the right key to unlock it, you can be truly happy again."

"Thank you, little sister,"

Then returning to the original topic of this call, "Don't forget to keep an eye out for James."

"I will. I can't wait for you to get out of there and come home. I know you've only been up there a few weeks, but I miss you."

"Soon. I'll try to get there for Thanksgiving."

"You better, or I'll hire a rescue helicopter to come get you."

More sisterly laughter before final good-nights and good-byes. "Hey, before we hang up let me talk to Dillon."

"Why?"

"I just want to say hi and goodnight."

"Seriously?" exasperated, Mysti hands the phone to Dillon. "My sister wants to talk to you."

Dillon smiles brightly taking the phone. "Hello?"

"Hi. Don't let on to my sister what I'm about to say to you. Got it?"

"Nice to meet you too," Dillon plays along.

"She has survived gut-wrenching heartbreak and the psycho that just called. Treat my sister kindly and with respect. Don't do anything to harm her physically or emotionally or I'll feed you to the three bears myself. Are we clear?"

Dillon continues to smile, "You sound like an amazing sister and Mysti is lucky to have you. I look forward to meeting you too."

"Cool. You catch on quickly. I think I like you already. Goodnight to you both," Autumn ends the call.

Casting Mysti a huge smile, Dillon sets the phone down.

"What did she say?"

"Not much. Just reminded me, as you often do, to be good to you or the boys will enjoy me as a treat. I'm exhausted, not sleepy yet, but ready to simply relax a bit. How about you?"

"Agreed."

They finish up their cocoa and popcorn while watching an episode of a singing competition on TV before crawling into bed.

Lying there in the darkness mentally rehashing earlier conversations, "Mysti? You still awake?"

"Yes."

"I was just thinking about how it's usually nice to find you have something in common with someone. However, I wish what we have in common neither of us had in our lives at all."

Mysti is confused, "Huh?"

"My Carla and your James. Two *crazies.*"

Mysti chuckles in the darkness. "Ooo! I have a great idea. We should introduce them. They can stalk each other!"

They both bust out laughing.

"Great idea."

They snuggle deeper into the covers and drift off to sleep smiling.

Dillon is wakened by Mysti's tossing and groaning. He can tell that she's having a bad dream. He doesn't want to wake her, so he just draws her safely into his arms and cuddles her close. Near instantly she succumbs to his comforting embrace.

"Jeff, oh I've missed you. Please don't leave me again."

Dillon's heart skips. Who's Jeff? Then he recalls Autumn's statement that Mysti has been through gut-wrenching heartbreak. Jeff must be who broke her heart.

~ 4 ~

"Hello," Cora answers the phone midday Tuesday.

"Hello, my name is Glenda Lubbers. Am I speaking to Cora?"

"Yes, this is Cora."

"I got your number from my son, Dillon, who got it from your daughter, Mysti. My son is the man whose life your daughter saved last week."

"Oh, hello. Yes, Mysti told me what happened when she called Friday night. I'm so glad she and the boys were up there and were able to rescue your son."

"My family and I are trying to put together a plan to get up there and bring them home. My husband has contacted the department of roads and transportation and they say that in the area our kids are it will be another week before they can get up there to clear the road."

"A week? Well, Mysti said they should have sufficient food and firewood to wait it out a while, but I'm not sure she was counting on it being another week."

"We aren't exactly sure where he is or was headed. His doctor loaned him his cabin for a few weeks. Do you know the area?"

"Yes, we also have a cabin just down the road from Mysti's. There is a village not far from her, just off the main road. They have some of their own plow equipment, but I doubt they know

76

the situation. I could try to get in touch with Josiah, but I'm not sure how much help that would be."

"We own *Land-Lubbers-Scaping* and we do private snow plowing in the winter. My husband and son think they can hitch our equipment trailer to the plow truck and plow their way up the mountain to find Dillon's car. Then find their way to your daughter's place to pick them up. If there is any plow help that can be done at that end it would be wonderful."

"I'll contact Josiah to fill him in on the situation so he can check with Paul who runs the village plow. My two sons would be more than willing to ride along with your husband and son to help dig out Dillon's car and anything else they can do to help. We own Van Strien Construction They're very strong boys."

"That would be great. The truck is a crew cab, so they can all ride together."

The two mothers exchange information and set the plan into action by contacting those involved.

Josiah contacts Paul to get him into action trying to clear the road from the village toward Cabin Ridge. Josiah also contacts Mrs. Waldeck, whom he checks in on more than once daily, and fills her in on the goings-on. And so, begins the game of telephone, also called the gossip mill.

Wednesday morning dawn breaks and the telephone rings. Dillon feels Mysti's whole body tense at the sound. He hugs her tighter. "I'll get it," he states emphatically as he releases her and clamors off the bed to answer it. He glances at the caller ID and realizes it's his mother's number.

"Good morning, Mom.... Yes, Mother, I'm still snowbound with Mysti...Yes, Mother, I'm behaving," Dillon listens as his mother proceeds to fill him in on the plans to rescue them.

"Your father and brother will be leaving shortly. They've off-loaded the skip loader from the trailer so they can load your car on it once they find and uncover it. They'll be picking up Mysti's brothers who are coming along to help. They're going to plow their way up the mountain so it won't be a quick, easy trip, however, Cora, Mysti's mother, has contacted a man named Josiah in the nearby village who in turn contacted the local plowman, Paul, who is in the process of plowing the road from the village toward the cabin."

Mysti has dressed and brought Dillon his clothes and is assisting him to dress, while his mother rambles on, before he nearly freezes again. She then stokes the fire while half listening in on his side of the conversation.

"Once they find your car, they'll dig it out, load it up and come pick up the two of you.

"The two of us?"

"Yes, Dear. You can't think for a moment that we'd leave the woman who saved our son's life stranded up there until who knows when? Besides, why else do you think her brothers are coming along?"

"No. It's just that there are five of us, remember?"

"Oh, well, yes. You did mention the dogs. Of course, they can come along too."

"The problem is we won't all fit in one vehicle even if her brothers weren't coming."

"Your father is bringing the Crew Cab truck, Dear. The dogs can sit on your laps."

Dillon chuckles. "They are definitely **not** lap dogs, Mom. Did you forget I told you they are big dogs? They weigh approximately 100, 150 and 200 pounds."

"What?" Glenda exclaims disbelievingly, "Are you teasing me, son?"

"No, Mother. They are massive. Their names are Polar, Grizzly and Kodiak for a reason. They each resemble their namesakes in looks and size."

"Oh, well, then... No wonder she felt safe having you stay there. You'd be no match for the three of them."

"And though I haven't met her brothers, judging by the XXXL sweatshirt that she loaned me the first night that belongs to one of them, I'm not sure even just the six people would fit in the truck.

"I was going to ask if the dogs could possibly ride in the bed of the truck if they were leashed but..."

"I don't think that would be a safe option anyway.

 Mysti has picked up the gist of the conversation from hearing Dillon's side of it.

"My dad, brother and your brothers are coming to get us?
"How?"

 "We own a landscaping business. Since there isn't much call for plants and gardening when it's snowing in the winter, we become a snowplowing company. We have a four-wheel drive crew cab diesel dually with front and rear plows," Dilon fills Mysti in on the plan.

"That's great. As I heard you explaining to your mom there's no way, we'll all fit in one vehicle. I drive an old four-wheel drive Suburban. It's in the barn. Maybe they can plow a path from my barn to the road and I can just follow you since you'll be clearing the road as you go. Then my brothers can ride back with the boys and me. That way we won't be inconveniencing you further."

"The only one inconveniencing anyone is me," his look is sheepish and contrite "That would solve the issue of where everyone would fit."

His mother has been listening to them work out a solution. "Let me speak to Mysti."

He hands Mysti the phone. "Hello?"

"I'm glad you figured out a solution to fit everyone. However, I want you to follow my family right back here to our house so I can properly thank you for saving my son's life. Do you hear me?"

"I hear you."

"Good. That's settled. May I please speak to my son again?"

Mysti hands the phone back.

After Dillon ends the call with his mother, he tells Mysti his mother's suggestion of the dogs sitting on laps and they have a good chuckle.

Mysti and Dillon pack up their belongings and Mysti begins a checklist of things to do before departure except for the last-minute stuff such as turning off the well pump and draining pipes so they won't freeze. Since it's daylight, she shuts down the generator, covers and locks it back up. She checks to be sure her Suburban will start after sitting in the cold barn for three weeks. It takes a few tries, but it starts. She lets it run to warm up all the fluids so it will run well on the drive down.

Mysti tells Dillon to call and inform the recovery team, "Mysti says she tied a long strip of fluorescent orange cloth as high up as she could reach on the highway snowplow post nearest to where she found my car. She hopes she tied it tight enough not to blow off and high enough it is still visible. She said it's about three-quarters of a mile before her driveway. The address to input into GPS is 11045 Osceola Route, Meadow Creek."

Dillon's twin brother, Dathan, has removed the rear plow in order to attach the trailer. He has loaded bricks on it at the axle line to help weigh it down to provide traction for the trailer tires. It will be helpful, but not great. He has the plow tilted as far to the right as possible to better clear the way.

Dathan and his father, Kip, arrive at Van Strien Construction to pick up Harlan and Hugh at 7:30 am, on their way out of town.

The four men introduce themselves. "Pleasure to meet you both," Harlan greets.

Kip states, "When my wife told me Dillon's impression that you two were rather large fellas, I had no idea you were quite this large. My boys and I are usually considered fairly good-sized, all at 6'2, but you two make me feel small," they all laugh amenably.

"Well, are we ready to go rescue the rescuers and the res-cued?" Hugh asks.

"That we are."

They make fairly good time, only 90 mins. the first 60 miles to get to the cutoff that takes them up the mountain, but then the going gets tough. The remaining 70 miles takes them four and a half hours, for a total of six hours just to make it to the village.

They pass through the village easily as Paul has cleared the main road of them. They finally see the orange flag Mysti sup-plied. Dathan pulls to the side of the road, but not off of it, since they don't want to get stuck and it's highly unlikely anyone will be passing by.

They trudge down into the ravine in search of Dillon's white car; like looking for the preverbal needle in the haystack. Twenty minutes later they locate the car.

"Wow, he really did go off the road," Dathan states.

Hugh says, Harlan and I will begin to uncover the car, while the two of you go about figuring the logistics of getting it hauled out."

It's determined they need to unhook the trailer and turn it around by hand, so it's facing downhill since there isn't room to maneuver it with the truck on this narrow snow-covered road.

Kip and Dathan start by unloading the bricks and putting them in the truck bed, then begin to carefully plow a path from the road toward the buried car. They get as close as they can. By then Hugh and Harlan have the car mostly uncovered. Dathan attaches the winch from the front of the truck and Kip begins to slowly drag the car back up to the road. Dathan, Hugh and Harlan assist by pushing the car from the front and occasionally from the side to keep it going straight. Forty-five minutes later the car is finally on the road, loaded onto the trailer and strapped down. They leave it on the side of the road with flares set.

"Now on to Mysti's place" Harlan states.

It's three o'clock when they arrive.

During the round of introductions, Kip asks, "So you felt the need to stay in keeping with the size of your brothers when acquiring dogs? Does your family do anything small?" They all laugh heartily.

"Nope. Pretty sure we don't."

Kip efficiently plows a path from the barn to the road making it possible for Mysti to get her Suburban out.

Mysti and Dillon have prepared a late lunch for their retrieval party. The six of them sit long enough to partake and replenish before heading out. The Lubbers load into the plow truck, the Van Striens and the three bears into Mysti's SUV. They stop to re-hitch the trailer, then depart to disembark the mountain. On the way down, they stop in town to fuel up and double-check trailer connections.

Mysti pops in to briefly tell Josiah what's up and finds Mrs. Waldeck sitting there with Josiah.

"There ain't been much business with this here storm soz when I dropped by to check on Ms. Waldeck and she mentioned being a bit bored, I offered for her to come sit a spell and visit," Josiah rushes to explain.

"Uh-huh. You don't need to explain yourselves to me. You're both consenting adults."

Mysti gives the couple a quick rendition of the rescue of Dillon, as well as the current recovery mission in progress. "I'll be gone a couple of weeks before returning to my cabin sanctuary."

"Don't you go forgettin' the Solstice Festival & Barn Dance," Josiah reminds Mysti

"I won't."

Dillon, Dathan, Kip, Hugh and Harlan have all popped in to grab some beverages and snacks for the road. Mrs. Waldeck and Josiah greet Hugh and Harlan warmly as they've known them longer than Mysti's been alive.

Mysti assists Dillon, carrying the items he intends to purchase.

The two elders observe Mysti's manner toward the gimp-legged fellow and make it known to each other with mere eye contact that they see...something.

Mrs. Waldeck asks, "Who are these fine gents."

Mysti makes introductions.

Josiah pipes up, "Ya otta bring the whole lot of 'em with ya to the festival and Barn dance, tho' it don't look like that one will be doin' any dancin' any time soon."

Kip asks, "What festival and barn dance might that be?"

Josiah is more than happy to fill them in on the festivities, times, etc....

"That sounds wonderful," I think we should bring the whole clan.

"The more, the merrier," Mrs. Waldeck assures. "How many are in your clan?"

Kip counts a moment silently before announcing, "Fourteen, if I counted correctly."

"That is a clan!" I look forward to meeting them all if you can make it."

'Your wayward stranger surly is easy on the eyes," Mrs. Waldeck's comments on Mysti's handsome rescue. Mysti rolls her eyes and sighs causing Mrs, Waldek to grin broadly. "You can't fool me, Mysti. That blush may not be visible to the naked eye but I can sense its presence."

Farewells are complete and the caravan, of sorts, gets back underway to continue down the mountain.

Once they reach the freeway, the drive is much clearer and easily traveled. Mysti remains following the Lubbers trio until she veers off onto the exit that will take her to their shop and ultimately home. She hadn't mentioned to Hugh and Harlan that she was expected to follow the Lubbers' to their house, so her maneuver doesn't seem unusual. They'd told her they'd left their trucks at the shop so she will drop them there before heading to her house.

As they round a curve of the freeway, Dillon glances back past the towed vehicle to be sure Mysti is still following but doesn't see her. "Hey, we lost them," he announces.

"She took an exit some ways back," Dathan informs.

"Why? Mom told her to come to the house so she can meet her."

"Maybe she and her brothers are just too tired. She still has to take them to their shop to get their vehicles. Plus, maybe the dogs are getting antsy to get out."

"But Mom wants to meet her," Dillon sounds suddenly depressed.

Kip looks back at his son and states in a fatherly knowing tone, "And you aren't ready to be separated."

Dillon doesn't respond, he looks back out the rear window half expecting to see them still behind them.

When the Lubbers men arrive at Dillon's parent's house, Glenda bolts out the front door heading straight to the rear driver-side door of the truck. Dillon is maneuvering his way out. He no sooner gets the foot of his good leg on the ground with both crutches in one hand before his mother throws her arms around him, hugging him tightly. Her tears of joy pouring forth. "Oh, Dillon I am so happy you are still alive," her words partially muffled against his jacketed shoulder. After long moments of hugging Glenda withdraws from the embrace looking past Dillon's trailered vehicle expecting to see another vehicle containing Mysti and her brothers.

At that moment Kip steps to her side answering her unspoken question. "I think everyone was tired. They took the exit toward their shop," he explains to his wife as Dillon makes his way toward the house. Kip and Dathan grace Glenda with smirks and knowing smiles in response to the quizzical expression she aims toward his son's dejected mood. Glenda responds with an eyebrow-raised look of curiosity, causing the two men to laugh outright as they follow Dillon to the house.

Inside Dillon discovers the rest of the family waiting to welcome his safe return. After hugging the safely returned one-third of her triplet set, Devan looks beyond him expecting to see his rescuer's entrance.

"She's not coming," he states somewhat glumly.

"Why Not?"

"How should I know? She just isn't."

Dathan pipes up. "It's not like it's the end of the world."

"I didn't say it was," Dillon snaps.

"Dill, all I'm saying is we'll get in touch with her and arrange something so we can all personally thank her for saving you. Mom has her mother's phone number, plus we know where their business is. Stop acting depressed, like you're never going to see her again."

"I'm not! I just know that Mom was expecting to meet her tonight."

Glenda covertly waves to Dathan and Devan to let it drop.

Dathan's wife, Danna hugs Dillon. "Darn good thing someone saved your uncle's hinny. I have no desire to have to find a baby-sitter as good as he is," Danna announces in a teasing manner. Her words directed to her two sons.

"No one could ever be as good a babysitter as Uncle Dillon."

"Uncle Dillon doesn't babysit us, he hangs out with us and *no* one could ever replace him," the boys state, hugging and bringing a smile to their Uncle.

"Yea, Uncle Dillon is the best uncle ever," Bridgit announces as she and her two younger siblings also hug their uncle.

The mood altered and uplifted slightly Danna announces, "We figured everyone might be hungry so there is a small buffet of food set up on the counter. Dig in."

Plates filled and everyone sitting scattered around the great room, Dillon's 12-year-old niece, Bridgit says, "Everyone has been saying you almost died. How?"

Dillon realizes he suddenly has everyone's attention focused on him and decides now is as good a time as any to explain, since the whole family is there. This way he'll only have to go through it once.

"I was saved from freezing to death by Sable Locks and the Three Bears," Dillon begins, catching the undivided attention of his nieces and nephews. In a tone of voice as if telling a spooky story, he begins;

"I was scared. I had crashed my car and couldn't get in un-stuck from the mounds of snow already on the ground. I stupidly decided to wander off to try make it the rest of the way on foot or at least to find help or shelter. The wind was howling, blow-ing the snow sideways. It was coming down like a blanket, not flakes. I didn't know which way to go. The snow became deeper. Too deep for me to walk even if I hadn't been on crutches. I fell deep into a mound of snow. I was unable to get up or even roll over. I had checked my watch just before I fell and had already been out of my car for nearly two hours. After I fell, I lay there in pain for a very long time. I kept calling out for help though I didn't think anyone would ever be able to hear me. I hadn't seen any signs of people for miles before the crash. I knew I had only enough strength for one last cry for help and I yelled as loud as I possibly could. Then I felt myself begin to fall asleep. I knew the worst thing to do was to sleep, but I was exhausted. Suddenly these two huge creatures came running toward me barking wildly. The biggest one stopped just before stepping on me. He sniffed me from head to toe then plopped right on top of me.

"He began breathing in my face. His doggy breath was hot and moist. It felt so good to feel warmth.

"The second beast ran back the way it had come, bringing back with him another beast and an Eskimo-looking being so bundled up I couldn't see the face. When the being spoke, I was shocked. I thought it was a man, but out from the fur-framed face came the sweet voice of a lady. I was sure she wouldn't be able to help me up, but she was as strong as any superhero.

"She loaded me on a toboggan that she hooked to the two smaller beasts. The big beast picked up and carried my full duffle bag with ease.

"When the lady got me back to her cabin and took off her parka hood, I saw her long flowing sable brown hair and looked at the three huge dogs that looked so much like bears, that's when I knew I'd been saved by Sable Locks and the Three Bears," Dillon tells the story as if telling them a fairytale bedtime story. The rest he tells with sincerity.

"There are some very important and valuable lessons for all of you, especially you kids, to learn from your uncle's incident. I don't want you guys," he looks pointedly at each child before continuing, "to become scared or overly upset, but I am going to be very honest about just how close I came to dying." Dillon explains the importance of having a plan and a backup plan and being prepared for any situation when setting out on an excursion, especially if you're alone. He also makes it clear to the children that even if someone thinks they are fully prepared, there are no absolute guarantees. He explains how very lucky he is that the dogs heard him as he knows that Mysti probably would never have heard him due to the howling wind and the sound muffling snow.

"I can't wait to meet Mysti and make sure she knows how grateful we are that she saved you. I don't think I could have handled it if you hadn't survived," Bridgit tells her uncle hugging him tightly, tears rolling down her cheeks.

The other children all agree, tearfully hugging their uncle.

After contacting Cora to get Mysti's cell number, Glenda calls Mysti.

"Hello."

"Good morning, Mysti. This is Dillon's mother. I hope I'm not interrupting anything."

"No, not at all. Is everything ok?" Mysti's voice is touched with concern.

"Yes, and no. I mean, Dillon is fine. However, you didn't come by last night. The whole family was here waiting to thank you."

"I... uh... I figured you needed family time to be with your son and I was tired, my brothers wanted to get home, the dogs needed to be let out...Besides you've already thanked me. It's all good."

"Kip, Dathan and I have, but the rest of the family wanted to express their gratitude in person. Can we find a time to all get together?"

Mysti hesitates thinking she can agree to a noncommittal *sometime* and in time they'll get over the idea and let it drop. "Yeah, sure we can probably find some time, but this week is busy for me with needing to attend to job site issues and Thanksgiving preparations and all. Then I'll be busy with the first of the month bookwork and payroll and I vowed not to miss the Solstice festival back up in Meadow Creek, then there's Christmas and New Year. Maybe after the first of the year, I can find time to stop by."

Glenda senses Mysti's avoidance ploy. She'll just have to change tactics. "OK, well, you do sound busy. I'm sure we'll figure out something. You take care, Dear."

"I will, you too. Please tell, um... your husband and son thank you for safe passage home."

"I will," Glenda senses Mysti had wanted to have her tell Dillon something, "Is there any message you'd like me to pass along to Dillon for you?"

"Oh, um, yeah, sure, I suppose. Uh, just tell him I'm glad he's back with family and to... behave so he can heal quickly. Thanks."

Noticing the apprehensive stutter and recognizing it as a tell-tale sign, Glenda smiles. "I'll tell him when I see him. We'll talk later. Bye for now," Glenda ends the call.

Snow falls throughout the afternoon and overnight, nothing to rival last week's storm, but a significant amount. Wally arrives at the job site to find the parking area not plowed and the crew unable to get on site to park and unload. Wally places a call to his private plow guy.

Rob's wife answers. "I am so sorry. I should have called you. Rob fell yesterday and we've spent the night at the hospital. He injured his back and is going to need surgery. He'll be out of commission until at least after the first of the year, probably more like the rest of the season. I'm so sorry."

"No, no, don't you be sorry. You tend to your husband. Give him our deepest sympathies and best wishes for a speedy recovery."

Wally stands there momentarily after hanging up trying to decide what to do. Suddenly remembering Lubber's family plow, he calls his wife. After filling her in on Rob's injury, he asks, "Could you call Glenda and see if her husband or son could come plow this morning?"

"Of course."

Cora places the call to Glenda who then calls Kip, passing on the request and contact information for him to call Wally directly.

"Sure thing. We'll be there in a bit," Kip assures.

Wally gives him the address.

Mysti arrives at the site a short while later to find Kip and Dathan there plowing.

"What is going on?" she asks her dad.

While Wally fills in all the details of the morning, Kip joins them.

"Good morning, Mr. Lubbers. Thank you for coming on such short notice. If you'll please tell me the cost for today, I'll go cut you a check immediately," Mysti greets stoicly.

"That won't be necessary. There is no charge for today. This is the least we can do for you and your family. We owe *you* our son's life. This is a mere token of gratitude for such a gift."

"I have no intention of taking advantage of your family. This is business. You have expenses which you incur to enable you to provide your services that need to be covered," Mysti speaks in a very business manner.

"We need to discuss the possibility of finishing out the season with you since it sounds like Rob is done for the year," Wally interjects.

Kip ponders a moment. "I'll tell you what. We'll take on your account for the season on the condition that today is no charge."

"Perfect. You have a deal," Wally responds looking to Mysti for her acceptance.

Mysti sighs heavily, "Fine, but enough with the *owing me* nonsense," she states walking off in a bit of a huff.

"My apologies for my daughter's mood."

"No apologies needed. My son's mood is quite similar. Makes one wonder..."

The two fathers exchange looks of curiosity and knowing smiles before following Mysti into the onsite office where she is preparing a contract for services. "What are your rates? Do Not understate them as I have means to check what others pay."

The business details are worked out and the contract is signed.

Dathan comes into the office just as Mysti asks in an off-handed manner, "How's Dillon?"

"Truthfully? Cranky and depressed. He says he's not but..."

"I'm sure in the aftermath of it all, it's a lot for him to render down. I know I woke last night from a nightmare of the *What if, alternate outcome.* It was scary for me. I'm sure it's horrifying for him. I think while we were still there, we were just living in the moment. Now that we're back to the *real world* the gravity of the experience is affecting us both."

"True. You've got a point," Kip agrees.

"Again, thank you for being available on such short notice today and for being able to fit us into your schedule for the season. I have things to attend to. Goodbye," Mysti gives her father a hug and peck on the cheek before they all depart the mobile office.

The three men watch her walk away. Once sure she is out of earshot, "Do you sense something? Or is it just me? I know I don't know your daughter, but I do know my brother and I sense... Attraction? Something...neither of them seems willing to confront."

 Both fathers agree that there is some underlying energy. Hugh and Harlan have just arrived on site and join the trio of men.

"What's this gossip group clucking about?" Hugh asks.
Dathan fills them in.

"Definitely," Harlan responds.

"I saw a glimmer of something when we arrived at the cabin. Their ease in the confines of the tiny kitchen, the secretly veiled glances they each thought the other and no one else noticed, but the tension Dillon emitted as soon as he realized she wasn't following us anymore? That was the kicker for me," Dathan offers.

At Hugh and Harlan's questioning expressions, Dathan explains, "She was supposed to follow us home where the whole family was waiting to thank her. "

"Ah! Our sister doesn't seem to like too much gratitude expressed toward her. Mysti says she does what should be done and what needs doing because everyone should. Mysti doesn't do anything for accolades. She does what she does because it's right."

"We as a family *need* to be allowed to express our appreciation for Dillon's life," Kip states emphatically.

Wally assures him, "We'll keep in touch and figure out some way to make it happen."

That evening Wally discusses the events and conversation of the morning with Cora.

"I'll come up with a plan," Cora assures.

That evening Kip discusses the events and conversation of the morning with Glenda.

"I'll come up with a plan," Glenda assures.

The following morning Cora is on the phone with her daughter, Autumn, discussing Thanksgiving Day preparations and chatting about the need to find a way for Dillon's family to meet Mysti.

The following morning Glenda is on the phone with her daughter, Devan, discussing Thanksgiving Day preparations and chatting about the need to find a way for the whole family to meet Mysti and thank her.

"I've got it!" Cora exclaims to Autumn.

"I've got it!" Glenda exclaims to Devan.

"Let me call you back. I have to make a call," Cora states, hanging up to dial Glenda's number.

"Let me call you back. I have to make a call," Glenda states, hanging up to dial Cora's number.

Cora clicks on Glenda's number just a moment faster and Glenda's phone rings as she is about to click on Cora's number. "Hello, Cora. I was just about to call you."

"I've got a wonderful idea!" Cora blurts out.

"I've got a fabulous idea!" Glenda proclaims.

The two women speak simultaneously, then laugh in unison.

Cora recovers first, "Since I obviously dialed first, I'll let you tell me your idea first."

"I was just on the phone discussing Thanksgiving Day plans with my daughter Devan. I *know* this is a lot to ask, but I'm wondering if maybe there is a way your family could *hog-tie* Mysti and you could all come to our house for Thanksgiving dinner or, at the very least, for dessert that evening?"

Cora laughs full out. Not the reaction Glenda is expecting.

Once Cora collects herself, she informs Glenda, "I was on the phone discussing Thanksgiving Day plans with my daughter Autumn. Here's my thought, I also *know* this is a lot to ask, but I think maybe there is a way your family could *hog-tie* Dillon, since he's injured it might be easier, and you could all come to our house for Thanksgiving dinner."

"Oh, my goodness. Great minds do think alike."

The two mothers hash out the details and decide Cora is right, it will be easier to get Dillon to their house since he has to be picked up because his car isn't repaired yet.

After the two mothers confirm their plans and end their call, they both attend to telling the two families, with oaths of secrecy vowed by all.

Dathan drops by Dillon's condo to pay him a visit on Sunday morning. He has a key, so he lets himself in calling out, "Dillon, it's me. Good morning, gimp. I didn't want you to have to get up," he greets, in explanation. Dathan finds Dillon on the couch with his laptop. "What's up, Brother?"

"Nothing much."

"Why are you holed up here like a hermit?"

"I was supposed to be in a secluded cabin in the mountains without distractions, writing for a few weeks. Since that all went haywire, I'm here writing as I intended. I'm just pretending I'm in seclusion. Well, until you shatter the illusion by waltzing in here unannounced and uninvited."

"Are you sure you're OK? I mean mentally, emotionally? We're all concerned about your state of mind."

Dillon inhales deeply, knowing his family means well, but unwilling to talk about the experience, yet. He knows they think he's only dealing with the freezing aspect of it all. Little do they know...

"Saw Mysti the other day."

"What?"

"She was saying even she's having nightmares about the possible alternate outcome. If this is affecting her that deeply, I know it's affecting you."

Dillon sighs heavily. "Yeah. You're right. I've been having dreams about the whole situation too."

Dathan smirks.

"What's that look for?"

"Dreams? Not nightmares?" Dathan asks.

"What?"

"There's a big difference between dreams and nightmares. You said dreams."

Dillon looks away, "Whatever. Same difference. "

"No, dear brother, not the same."

"Drop it!" Dillon replies grumpily.

Dathan decides not to push it.

"Hey, Dill. I'm here for you brother. Whenever you're ready to talk and you *need* to talk, you can't bottle up and hide away the emotions of the experience. It's not healthy."

"I'm fine!" Dillon snaps.

"Remember who you're talking to. Devan and I are both going through this aftermath with you. Our triplet connection is too strong for you to overlook. We weren't with you, but we're dealing with the aftermath of the *what could have.* You need to allow us all to celebrate with you the *what did* and thankfully, not dwell on the *what could have....*"

"I hear you. I just..."

"Just what?"

"I wish Mysti would have come, so the whole family could have met her and thanked her. I wanted her to see all the people whose lives she saved by saving mine. I know it would have meant a lot to Mom."

"And you like her and miss her," Dathan states as fact.

"No! I'm sure it's just some psychological syndrome someone gets toward the person who rescues them. That's all." Changing the subject, he continues. "By the way, where, when and why did you see Mysti?"

"That's right Mr. Hermit, you don't know," Dathan tells Dillon about the urgent call for plowing.

The next few days fly in a hectic flurry of activity and preparations for Thanksgiving Day.

On Monday Dillon asks his sister Kayla to drive him to go see Dr. Barton to return his unused cabin key and fill him in on the escapades.

While Dillon relays all the details of the events that he endured, Dr. Barton uses his computer to schedule an urgent MRI.

While watching Dillon as he retells the ordeal, Doc notices a difference in his patient who is also a longtime friend.

"I need you to go down and do the MRI I just scheduled so I can see if your adventure re-injured my repairs or did any further damage to your leg."

"When?"

"They'll be ready for you in twenty minutes. By the way, you know you now owe this Mysti a lifetime of servitude as gratitude," Doc jokes, but sees Dillon's immediate posture change and quick inhaled breath.

"Is that true? I mean, is that just a myth or is that like a real thing?"

Doc isn't quite sure if his pal appears horrified or hopeful at the thought of being beholding to Mysti and says as much. "Would that be a good thing or a bad thing?"

Dillon tries and fails to hide the flushed expression and glimmer of delight that thought sparks before turning away.

Doc Barton chuckles.

"What's so funny?"

"Nothing, but you know Dillon, I think maybe you should have your eyes checked."

"Why?"

"Because they look different since the last time I saw you."

"You mean like some kind of damage from nearly freezing to death?"

"Nope. I see something different, like a twinkle of happiness."

Dillon graces the Dr. with a scowl. "I think you need to pay a visit to one of your colleagues because I think your 'humorous' is broken."

Doc grabs Dillon's arm and examines it lightly.

"Now what?"

"No, my Humerus is fine, it's your funny bone that's broken."

Dillon picks up his crutches, "I should get going so I don't miss my MRI appointment."

"Good idea. Here's another good idea. I'd like to meet Mysti and personally thank her for taking such good care of you, my friend."

"I don't see that happening. She wouldn't even come to my parents to let the family thank her."

"Maybe in time."

"Later, Doc."

"I'll let you know if I see anything of concern when I get the MRI results later this week."

Dathan calls Dillon Wednesday evening, "Hey, brother. I'm going to come pick you up around 1:00 or 1:15 tomorrow. Dinner is scheduled to begin at 2:30. Oh, Mom asked everyone to dress extra nice this year."

"Why?"

"You know Mom. We always dress decent, but she just wants this year to be even more special since..." Dathan let the explanation hang.

"Whatever. It's no more special than every other year, but if it makes Mom happy."

"Good. I was hoping you'd abide her wishes. See you tomorrow."

"Bye."

Dillon pulls out his Brown suit, peach dress shirt and tri-color striped tie. He sprays the suit and tie with fabric freshener to eliminate the musty smell from them being in the closet for so long and irons the shirt.

Thanksgiving morning sun rises brightly. Dillon has his morning coffee and bowl of cereal, showers and dresses, and is ready and waiting when Dathan arrives at 1:10.

Glenda has prepared all the food she would have for her own family the night before with the help of Danna and Devan.

Thanksgiving morning Kip helps Glenda load everything into their SUV and makes sure everything is securely wedged for the drive.

Glenda pulls up the text containing the address Cora sent. Clicking it to open in maps to receive directions. "Searching for directions to 2026 Big Dalton," the map app's assistive voice announces as they head out the driveway.

Cora has prepared all the food she normally does for her own family. Realizing the large number of people that will be descending on this meal they've set up everything in buffet style.

Thanksgiving morning's sun rises brightly. Dillon has his morning coffee and bowl of cereal, showers and dresses, and is ready and waiting when Dathan arrives at 1:10.

Devan meets her parents at the Van Strien home leaving her husband, Tyce, to wrangle, dress and bring their three children. Since Dathan is in charge of picking up Dillon, Danna and their two boys are meeting everyone else at the Van Strien house at one o'clock.

Kayla and Kiersten arrive right as Danna plus two, Tyce plus three, Autumn, Hugh and Harlan all arrive "Perfect timing," Devan remarks as everyone, near simultaneously, disembark their vehicles.

"You must all be Dillon's family," Harlan observes.

Everyone quickly pitches in to hurriedly get everything and everyone in the house before Mysti or Dillon arrive, then all the Lubbers' family vehicles are re-parked around the corner so the extra number would not be noticed by Mysti or recognized by Dillon. So far, the timing is going according to plan.

Introductions are just finished being made when Bridgit announces from her self-appointed position as lookout, "Uncle Dillon and Uncle Dathan just pulled up."

Everyone becomes quiet as most go to the window to discreetly observed how Dathan is going to convince Dillon to hobble into this unfamiliar house.

"Where are we?"

"You ask too many questions. Just hobble your gimpy self out of the truck and into the house and all your questions will be answered, but you need to hurry."

"Why?"

"For once in your life can you please just do as you're told?"

"You're up to something."

"You're right. Now hurry up and get in the house before you mess up everything."

Dillon finally complies. He is greeted by a heartwarming chorus of "Surprise!" "Happy Thanksgiving!" as he is quickly ushered into the living room.

Cora quietly explains, "Mysti should be here any minute. Everyone, stay quiet. Hi, I'm Cora, Mysti's mom. Welcome," she greets hugging Dillon.

Dillon looks around taking in the fact that his entire family is standing in this strange house that he can only now assume is Mysti's parents' home. The pieces of the puzzle begin to quickly fall into place and he realizes this is all intended to surprise, aka trick, Mysti into meeting his grateful family.

"She's here and as expected she brought the boys. Hold on to the little ones, so they don't get knocked over," Autumn announces from near the front door. Then turns on the video feature of her phone to document the impending event.

The door opens and in bounds the three massive canines followed by Mysti, who closes the door before turning to see the crowd and hear the second rendition of the chorus of "Surprise!" "Happy Thanksgiving!" Mysti stands staring dumbfoundedly. The three bears have already begun making their greeting rounds to those they know and new friends alike.

Mysti's mind races trying to make sense of what she is seeing. Recognition strikes when she catches sight of first Kip and Dathan, then she sees Dillon standing off to the side looking almost as shocked as she feels.

Cora steps to her daughter, wrapping her arms around her, before quickly letting go to allow another mother to wrap her grateful arms around Mysti.

The woman's hug is tight and sincere, lasting much longer than would be expected of a stranger. Mysti hears the woman sniffle before loosening her grasp slightly and raising her face and eyes to look directly into Mysti's suddenly moisture-filled eyes.

"Thank you... Those words will never be sufficient to express my most sincere gratitude for you saving my son."

Mysti can no longer hold back the flood of tears. Nor can the woman, who lets go of Mysti, allowing one after the other from the line that has formed behind her to in turn take Mysti into their arms to express their gratitude.

In the recesses of Mysti's mind, she hears a teasing voice question, "Does the line end?"

Mysti's mind registers that she is being hugged by children too, who like the adults, are also crying.

Moments after Mysti thinks the line of huggers is complete, Cora states as Mysti's own family begins taking their turn expressing their love and joy, "How blessed you are, my dear Mysti, to have been gifted this opportunity to express the unselfish love the Universe expects of us all."

Mysti stands there still feeling very shocked. Everyone else seems to step aside until the only face Mysti sees is that of the handsome gimp standing there. A myriad of expressions crossing his features to settle into a smirk.

Dathan pipes up breaking the spell that has befallen the room. "Are you going to be the only person here *not* to give *your* rescuer a hug of gratitude?"

"Yeah, Uncle Dillon. What's up with that?" Bridgit joins Uncle Dathan in joking.

Finally, Dillon hobbles toward Mysti who meets him halfway, for an awkward quick hug.

Wally calls out loudly, "Who's hungry?" to which a harmonized affirmative response erupts as everyone makes their way toward the dining room where a massive spread of food awaits.

Dillon and Mysti stand rooted for moments longer. Dillon whispers for her ears only, "I am as shocked and unaware of this whole scheme as you are. I literally arrived less than five minutes before you and had no idea where or why until Dathan commanded me to come in the house. I received the same initial surprise greeting."

In unison, they state, "My mom," they giggle softly.

Mysti imparts, "With the scope of this, I have a feeling they were all in on it."

"Agreed. Shall we," Dillon gestures the direction the others have gone.

The remainder of the day is a boisterously joy-filled event, with enough food to feed a large army. After dinner, Mysti and the children enjoy romping in the snow with Kodiak, Polar and Grizzly. Mysti has a great time getting to know the children. Bridgit, the eldest, tells Mysti how close they all are with their Uncle Dillon. "He's like our only babysitter. We all have so much fun with him."

The play has dwindled and all five kids are gathered around Mysti snuggling the dogs while they talk.

"Which one was first to get to Uncle Dillon?" Elton asks.

"It was probably Polar, with Kodiak mere steps behind. Kodiak is the one who acted like a blanket. He laid on top of your uncle to begin raising his body temperature, keeping him from freezing."

All five children hug Kodiak sincerely, grateful for his part in saving their uncle. They then each take turns hugging the other two dogs, "Thank you all for keeping the best Uncle in the world alive and bringing him back to us," Brooke tells them.

Mysti is squatting down to the height of the kids and dogs. Parker, the youngest, throws his arms around Mysti's neck hugging her more tightly than she recalls ever being hugged. Parker places a long warm smooch on Mysti's cold cheek before pulling back to look Mysti in the eyes, "You are our superhero. We will love you forever. You are part of our family now and forever."

"Yea, you're Super Hero Sable Locks and the Three bears," Bridgit announces.

"What? Where did you come up with that?" Mysti inquires.

"When Uncle Dillon told us about you guys saving him, he said he was saved by Sable Locks and the Three Bears," Elton explains.

"Because you live in the forest like Goldie Locks," Elias adds.

"But your hair isn't gold, it's sable brown," Brooke clarifies.

"Instead of you just visiting the three bears you all live together now," Bridgit concludes.

"Yeah, that's right," Elias agrees. After a few more hugs for the dogs, they all go back in the house.

Football games play on the big screen in the den. Conversations are lively as everyone gets to know each other.

Mysti tells about Dillon not having a dry shirt the first night. "When he put on Hugh's sweatshirt the thought that crossed my mind was Honey, I Shrunk the Kids."

Everyone laughs.

Autumn decides now is as good a time as any to ask the question that has been rumbling in her mind since she first heard about this whole ordeal. "I have a question."

Those in earshot become quiet to allow her question to be heard. Autumn looks directly at her sister, then at Dillon. "Mysti's cabin doesn't have a couch, and there is only one bed. Where did the two of you sleep?"

Silence envelopes the room, broken only by the sounds of children playing in the other room and referee whistles on TV in the den.

Mysti looks directly into her sister's mirth-filled eyes. "Being that we are both mature adults, and my bodyguards were with me at all times, we shared the one king-sized bed."

Seemingly right on cue the three bears amble into the living room and plop at Mysti's feet. Everyone chuckles.

"Desert anyone?" Cora inquires.

Coffee and Apple pie ala mode is served before Dathan's and Devan's families begin packing up to head home.

"It's kind of early for you to go. You should stay. I'm sure someone will take you home," Dathan tells Dillon as he makes to leave.

"I'll have Mom or Dad take me home."

Kip calls from across the room before anyone has the chance to leave, "Hey, Mysti. You still planning to go back up for that festival Josiah was telling us about?"

"Of course. I go every year. It celebrates my favorite holiday, Winter Solstice."

"I looked up the festival online to see what kinds of activities it has and I think it will be an amazing experience for everyone. They have snowman building contests, snow fort building with snowball challenges, food booths, arts and crafts for sale, as well as nature crafts and Solstice Eve activities. As well as a true barn dance. I think we should all go, especially since the founder of the event himself invited me to bring the whole clan."

"I agree everyone would probably enjoy it. However, it is a two-day event and there aren't many accommodations available near there, so it might not..." Mysti

"Well, if everyone is ok with bunking close together, I'm sure most of us can fit at our cabin and have a slumber party. Our cabin is much larger than Mysti's place. We have three bedrooms with beds and bunks, two sofa beds and two recliners," Wally interrupts his daughter.

"That sounds wonderful," Glenda affirms. "When is it exactly?"

"Solstice is the 21st so this year's event is the weekend of December 19th and 20th." Mysti supplies.

"Sounds amazing. I say we do it," Danna agrees.

"OK then, we'll keep in touch to finalize plans for carpooling, food, etc...." Glenda says as farewells begin for this day.

Mysti glimpses Kiersten smiling coyly at Harlan, whose ruddy complexion tells tales on him. Mysti catches Dillon's eye and nods toward the pair talking off to the side of the farewell commotion. Mysti and Dillon share an amused, knowing smile.

On the drive taking Dillon home, Glenda states, "Mysti seems to be very well rounded, caring, self-assured. All in all, a wonderful young lady."

"After meeting her family it's easy to see, how could she be otherwise?" Kip agrees.

"I'm glad you figured out a way for everyone to meet and thank her. However, it would have been nice if you'd warned me."

"What fun would that have been?" Glenda responds, a mischievous lilt in her voice. Dillon sees his father sneak a glance in the rear view mirror and notes the smirk on his father's face.

~ 5 ~

Mysti walks briskly into her favorite neighborhood restaurant to pick up her to-go lunch order. "Hey, Suzy. How's it going?" she greets the longtime hostess and lifelong friend.

Mysti's attention is then caught by the giggle coming from the young woman standing in the waiting area with her hand on the forearm of the man on crutches she is with. The woman looks up just then and seeing Mysti looking their way, smiles. The man turns to see who his companion is smiling at and hears Suzy's response to the woman moments before greeting.

"Hi, Mysti. Going great. Your order is almost ready," Suzy announces as she takes in the scene unfolding. Suzy not only sees but is near enough to hear Mysti's sharp inhale as the man turns, obvious recognition evident on both faces.

"Mysti? Hey. Small world," Dillon recovers first.

"*The* Mysti?" His female companion inquires recognizing the name.

"Yes, *The* Mysti," he responds, smiling.

Without hesitation the young woman withdraws the hand from Dillon's forearm and directly approaches Mysti, pausing squarely before her before wrapping her arms around Mysti in a heartfelt hug of appreciation. "Thank you for saving Dill. I am forever grateful. Life without Dilly in it would be no life at all."

Hearing the woman's use of nicknames, Mysti swallows hard. As the woman withdraws from the embrace, Mysti stammers, "Uh, yea, no problem. Glad to have been of service."

Dillon has come nearer, "Mysti this is Jessie..." he begins.

"Nice to meet you. Um...I have to get my order and get going. You know, umm...back to work, and, uh...bye," she turns back to the hostess, handing her the money to pay for her order. "Thanks, Suzy. See you next time," she grabs the bags of food and leaves quickly, leaving the other two women and Dillon looking from one to the other in puzzlement.

Just then Kayla comes through the door. "Hey, big brother, I think I just saw Mysti urgently run out of here. Did you happen to see her? Is everything ok?"

Jessie answers for them, "Yea, that was weird. She saw us standing here. When Dill greeted her and I realized who she was, I gave her a hug and thanked her for saving this guy and it seems she couldn't get out of here fast enough."

Kayla looks at her brother who still appears confused. Kayla laughs outright.

"What's so funny?" Jessie asks.

"Yea, what are you laughing at?"

Kayla contains her laughter long enough to reply, "You and Mysti? That's what."

Understanding strikes Jessie who joins Kayla in laughter. "I get it. She thinks... Oh, little does she know... She thought... but me and Dillon? ... This is hysterical..." Jessie tries to voice her sudden comprehension while laughing.

Kayla continues to laugh along until seeing Dillon's disapproving glare. "I'm sorry," she apologizes collecting herself and stifling her mirth.

"She claims she's going back to work? Who works the day after Thanksgiving?" Jessie asks.

"Apparently, Mysti," Dillon states.

Suzy, nonplussed, watches the scene taking place and overhears what is said. She thinks these three are laughing *at* Mysti. Suddenly feeling protective of her friend, she asks in a not so gracious hostess tone, "If you're finished with your immature games, I'll assume you'd like a table for three?"

Not understanding what the hostess means by her statement Dillon chooses to let it slide. "Yes, Please. Thank you."

"This way."

After being seated Kayla observes, "I wonder what bit her? She's usually very polite."

"It's the holiday season. A lot of people get overwhelmed this time of year," Jessie comments as the trio goes about menu selection.

"I came over as soon as my shift ended," Suzy explains to Mysti when she arrives at the onsite office.

"Why? What's up?"

"That's what I came to ask you."

"What do you mean?"

"That incident when you came to pick up your lunch. You looked so upset and nearly ran out of there. Very unlike you. Then after you left another woman came in and met up with that couple and they were talking and laughing so hard I couldn't catch all they were saying, but it sounded like they were laughing at you. I caught something about 'She thought she, but me and Dillon? That's hysterical.' It felt and sounded like you'd just found out you're the *other woman* in that guy's life. Are you OK?"

"Oh, no, Suzy. It's nothing like that," Mysti tries to think of an alternate reason for her hasty departure. "That was Dillon. He's the guy I rescued last week in the blizzard while I was up at my cabin."

"What?"

"Everyone keeps making such a big deal about it and I'm just not comfortable with all the attention, so I just wanted to get away quickly. That's all."

Suzy watches her friend's expression and senses that is only a half-truth. "That doesn't explain the conversation that followed."

"I wasn't there, so I have no clue what they talked about. It probably had nothing to do with me."

"Well, I thought you should know that, as well as that the guy didn't look pleased that they were laughing and he watched your departure intently. There was a moment I thought he was going to hobble after you."

"Good thing he didn't. He'd never have caught me," Mysti tries to make light of it all. "Thanks for your friendship, Suzy. I appreciate your concern."

Suzy asks for the low down on the rescue. Mysti gives her the cliffnote version. Seeming satisfied Suzy hugs her friend good-bye, "See you next time you come grab lunch."

It's late Sunday morning and Dillon is sitting at his computer working on his book when his phone rings.

"Hey, Brad. How are you?"

"Hey, buddy what's up? I'm fine. Are you busy? Mind if I stop by?"

"No, not busy, sure you can stop by."

"Good, since I'm at your front door," Brad chuckles, "Mind if I let myself in?"

Dillon hears the front door open before he can even answer. He ends the call turning his desk chair to witness his best friend enter.

"Why bother calling and asking? When you intend to let yourself in any way," Dillon joshes.

"Glad to see you're obeying doctor's orders and staying off your leg. How's it feeling?"

"It feels pretty good and yes, I am trying to obey my doctor's orders, especially after last week. By the way, did you get the results of the MRI?"

"Yes, everything seems to be healing quite well. I want you to start doing some physical therapy next week. You may start putting slight weight on that leg when you walk while still supported by the crutches for now. With the ordeal you went through I'm surprised there wasn't further damage."

"Yeah, I was concerned I had really done a number on it with all the trudging through the snow. Glad I didn't. I'm having a hard time staying down as it is, wouldn't want to have to add more duration to my being laid up."

"I have a question for you. Do you know anything about Windows?"

"Not much, why?"

"Since the temperature was a bit warmer earlier today, I decided to open a window in my office at my house and let some fresh air in. I heard a strange sound when I did, but didn't think much of it. When I tried to close it, it won't. I tried everything. I don't want to break the glass. Any suggestions?"

"I suppose I could go over with you and take a look at it. I know landscaping, I'm not much of a handyman, but I might be able to figure it out."

Dillon grabs his coat and they head out. Dillon takes a look at the window and realizes he knows nothing about this type of window.

"Know anyone that might know something about Windows?"

"Actually, I do," Dillon pulls out his cell phone and calls Mysti's number.

"Hello."

"Hi, Misty. This is Dillon. How are you?"

"Fine."

"Are you busy?"

"Just writing."

"I was too until a friend dropped by. He has an issue with a window at his house. He opened it earlier today and now can't get it to close. He wondered if I knew anyone that could help. I thought of you. Any suggestions?"

"Not without seeing it. What's the address? I'll go check it out."

"Are you sure? I mean it is Sunday and it is a holiday weekend. I didn't mean for you to have to work. I just thought maybe you had a suggestion."

"It's not a big deal. Just tell me where I'm heading."

"I'll text you the address. Thank you so much."

"What's your friend's name?"

"Brad."

"Okay, bye."

Misty changes out of the comfy sweats she wears while home writing before heading out.

Brad answers the door to find Misty standing with her toolbelt slung over her shoulder and carrying a toolbox as well.

"Well, you look like you came prepared. Hi, my name is Brad. Welcome," he greets as he steps aside allowing her to enter his home.

"Nice to meet you, Sir. My name is Misty, I received a call from your friend Dillon that you have an issue with a window not closing."

"Yes."

A sound off to the side catches Misty's attention. Instinctively glancing to see what caused the sound Misty inhales sharply at the site of Dillon standing there. "You?"

"Didn't I mention I was here?"

"It seems you omitted that bit of information."

Brad observes the interaction between these two, barely able to conceal his smirk, "Is there a problem with him being here?"

"No, it's just that he said he was writing. I wasn't expecting him to be here."

"As I recall, you also said you were writing, but you're not now, either."

"Yeah, well, that's because this guy called and asked for help for a friend of his."

"Yeah, well, my friend asked for my help and I tried and failed. That's why I called in knowledgeable reinforcements."

"Whatever," Misty turns to Brad, "Where's the window?"

"This way," Brad leads Misty to his office. Dillon remains in the living room.

"I'm sorry to disturb you on the weekend let alone a holiday weekend. I'll pay you for your time."

"Don't worry about it. As I said, I've been writing all day, this is a welcome break."

Mysti checks out the situation with the window. "These are old-style double-hung sash windows. The wood is deteriorating. Some of it broke away causing the clip end of the pulley to come free and lodge in between the window frame and the casing preventing the window from moving."

"Wow! Okay, glad you know what's wrong. Next question, can you fix it?"

"Of course. Do you have an old sheet or large towel I can place on the floor to prevent getting debris everywhere?"

"I'll find something. Be right back."

Mysti sets about getting out the tools she'll need.

Brad finds Dillon standing near the hallway entrance. Grabbing a sheet from the hall linen closet, Brad shoots Dillon a surprised, impressed look. "She seems to really know her stuff."

"I'm not surprised. She's a pretty impressive lady."

"Did you mean pretty impressive or pretty, impressive?" Brad smirks as he continues on to deliver the bedsheet.

Mysti takes the sheet and lays it out as a drop cloth to catch the wood fragments that are sure to fall. She then sets about removing the trim pieces to enable her to remove the lower portion of the window.

Dillon has quietly come to the doorway to stand with Brad watching Mysti in action.

Once the trim pieces are removed and the pulley is dislodged, Misty goes about removing the whole pulley mechanism. Sensing the two men observing her every move, she explains, "This will allow you to close the window. If you want it open, you will have to prop it with a stick or some other item for now, at least until I can order you a new pulley mechanism. I'll have to bring back some wood putty to help restructure the damaged wood where the clip is required to be placed. Other options would be to have new window frames milled to fit this casing or have all new windows installed. Both of those options are much more expensive and lengthier projects. With this one being this damaged there are probably others in similar condition that may go at any time. You'll need to be careful when opening any of them."

Misty replaces the window; carefully replaces the trim she's removed then begins cleaning up the debris and her tools. Brad asks, "How much do I owe you for today?"

"Nothing. It's fine. I'm just glad I was available and able to help. It would be pretty darn cold in here tonight when the temps drop with this still open."

"At least let me buy you dinner. You like pizza?"

"Who doesn't?"

"I'm hungry and I'm sure both you and Dillon are as well. If you don't have other plans, I'll order pizza. You can hang out here with us for a while. Besides, I also owe you for saving this guy's life and taking such good care of my patient," Brad good-naturedly elbow jabs Dillon in the ribs.

"Patient? You mean, you're his doctor?"

"I take it he forgot to mention that as well. You know Dillon, if this forgetfulness keeps up, I may have to have you tested for Alzheimer's," Brad teases.

"It's not so much forgetfulness, more omission of unnecessary or unimportant information."

"Are you saying I'm unimportant?" Brad asks teasingly. "Was I unimportant when you needed your leg repaired? Or the multitude of other times I have helped you out of jams?"

"I didn't say you were unimportant just that I didn't feel it was important to tell her who you were when I was requesting her assistance."

"What's your excuse for not telling her you were here when you asked for her assistance?"

Dillon shrugs, letting that one drop, he returns to the living room followed by Brad and Misty who has completed her cleanup.

"What do you like on your pizza?" Brad asks as he picks up his cell phone to place the order.

"I'm vegetarian, so most any vegetables, except mushrooms, is fine with me," Misty responds.

Brad looks to Dillon for his response. "That sounds great to me as well."

Dillon sees the squinted eye look of curiosity directed at him by his longtime friend. "Vegetarian minus mushrooms it is."

"You don't both have to eat vegetarian style on account of me. You can have them just do one-quarter of the pizza, vegetarian style or I can order a small for myself."

"Nonsense. I said I'm buying. It's not like it will hurt either of us to go without meat. I'm sure while Dillon was stranded with you, you didn't feed him meat and he looks no worse for wear."

Brad asks what beverages they each would like and completes the online order for delivery.

Misty begins to feel a bit uncomfortable and questions herself as to why she agreed to stay and eat. She decides to excuse herself to return her tools to her truck.

Turning to Dillon after Misty closes the door behind her, Brad asks, "What's going on between you two?"

"What do you mean? There's nothing between us."

"You can lie to yourself, but my eyes and senses do not lie to me."

"Whatever, Doc."

"I'm just saying if the tension between you gets any thicker, I may need to cut it with my scalpel."

Mysti re-enters in time to hear Dillon say, "Zip it, Doc."

Brad laughs.

"Did I miss a good joke?"

"No, my Doc was merely being his obnoxious self," Dillon answers while gracing his friend with a look that says to keep his thoughts to himself.

While they wait for the pizza to arrive, Mysti and Brad discuss his window options.

"I bought this place four months ago, with the intention of doing quite a bit of renovating to make it my own. I know it needs a lot of work. Obviously, I know nothing about it and had planned to research and hire someone knowledgeable. Is this type of renovation in the scope of what your family's company does?"

"Of course." Mysti looks around as they talk. "From what I can see on the surface, it appears the house has good bones. It could be restored or remodeled depending on your style."

"I am thinking I'd like to restore and update. Like install all new energy efficient windows but that still look like what's here now."

"Sounds great. That would have been my suggestion. The house has such a quaint charm. I wouldn't want to ruin that. If you're interested in giving our company a crack at it, why don't you jot down some of your ideas and we can schedule an appointment to do a full walkthrough and give you a bid."

"Perfect."

The doorbell rings signaling the arrival of the pizza. Brad goes to get it.

"Seems the two of you are getting along quite well," Dillon states to Mysti.

"What's that supposed to mean?"

"Nothing. Just an observation."

"One that smacks of sarcasm."

"I wasn't being sarcastic. Merely making a statement."

"We're discussing business. You do recall, you're the one who called me to come help. If it's going to bother you for me to work for him, say so now and I'll leave."

"Leave? You're not leaving now. The pizza just got here," Brad sounds puzzled reentering the conversation.

Not acknowledging Brad's interjection, Mysti continues, "As for our 'getting along quite well', you should talk. It's not like we're giggling and getting all touchy-feely in public."

"What? What are you talking... OH! So that's why you stormed off the other day. Kayla was right."

"I think I missed something here," Brad half mumbles while standing there holding the pizza trying to figure out what is going on. "Pizza anyone?"

"I should go."

"No!" Brad states emphatically. "You two are going to sit down like the mature adults you're supposed to be and eat while calmly discussing whatever the heck is causing this rift."

Brad looks from one to the other. "Sit!" he commands. They sheepishly obey.

Once everyone is seated and served, "Now would one of you like to explain to me what the heck is wrong with you two?"

"Your friend here was commenting on how well you and I are getting along, his tone smacking of sarcasm and jealousy."

"I'm not the one who ran out of the restaurant. That was you who did the other day when you saw me talking to my sister's friend."

"I didn't run out of the restaurant. I was in a hurry. Besides, you and your *sister's friend* looked awfully cozy."

"Jessie and Kayla have been friends since they were three years old. I've known Jessie most of her life. She's like another sister. Were you jealous? Is that why you've barely spoken to me today?"

Brad's sudden outburst of laughter catches both Dillon and Misty off guard. "You should hear yourselves. You sound like an old jealous married couple."

"Jealous?" Misty and Dillon speak in unison causing Brad to laugh even harder.

"That one-word reaction is the most harmonic thing that has taken place between the two of you since Mysti's arrival today. For two people who say nothing is going on between them, you sure seem to have issues with what the other one says or does."

Both Dillon and Misty go about eating in silence. Neither willing to respond to that.

"I'm thinking hiring Mysti is as good a way as any to thank her for saving your sorry butt. If it's going to bother you for me to have Mysti work for me, speak now."

"No, of course, I don't mind her working for you. You can hire whomever you want."

"As long as all that goes on between us is business, right? And just to be clear, I wasn't asking for your permission to hire her, merely asking you to tell me if I'm going to have to put up with this jealousy the whole time."

"Yes, I mean. No, I mean... It's none of my business if you two do business together. Or whatever. I'm not...there is no jealousy."

"Right. Ok then. That's settled." Brad chuckles under his breath, "At least for now."

Brad turns the topic of conversation back to the renovation. This time Dillon joins in and shares ideas.

Two comfortable conversation hours later, Mysti announces, "I should be getting home."

"It's been great hanging out with and getting to know you. I look forward to working together. I think you see my vision for this house. Again, thank you for saving and caring for this pain in the rear," Brad shoulder hugs Dillon. "A lot of people would have been devastated had there been a different outcome to his adventure."

"As I keep telling everyone, it was no big deal. I did what needed doing as would anyone in the same situation. I'm glad I was there to be of service... most of the time," Mysti ribs Dillon.

Brad catches the teasing in her tone. With a wink, "I'm right there with you on that."

"Great friend you are," Dillon tries to sound wounded by their teasing comments.

"Mysti, I know I have no right to impose on you any further, but since you're already going out, is there any way I could get you to drive gimpy home for me?"

Mysti feigns distressed imposition, sighing heavily, "I suppose I could be put upon to rescue him, yet again," then in a normal tone, "Of course. There's no reason for you to go out when I'm capable of taking him on my way."

"Gee, thanks. Sorry for being such an imposition on you both," It's Dillon's turn to feign distress.

Moments later they depart. Brad closes the door before allowing himself to once again laugh at the pair, "Oh boy, they've both got it bad."

Dillon tells Mysti where he lives, "You live a bit beyond my house. Would you mind terribly if I stop home and let the boys out? I've been gone much longer than I anticipated. I usually leave them out in the yard, but I thought I'd be right back."

"Of course, I don't mind, as long as you allow me to say hi to them."

"Sure, they'd probably like that."

"I know they have thick enough coats to be left out, but do you ever worry about them being out too long or someone turning you in for leaving them out?"

"Nope. They have their own enclosed patio room with a doggie door, bedding, food and water to go into to protect them from the elements, even though Kodiak and Polar usually choose to remain outside due to their winter coats. Grizzly's coat isn't quite as thick because he's half Rottweiler and he has short hair with no undercoat, so he hangs out in the dog room more than the other two."

After a brief excited greeting, one that nearly knocks Dillon over, Mysti and Dillon stand watching the three bears romp in the snow in Mysti's large backyard.

Dillon clears his throat, "About what I said earlier, I didn't mean to sound...I mean, I don't know why what I said sounded so...I, I mean I have no right or reason to be jealous. That's not like me. If I were in a relationship and my partner's interest was elsewhere, I'd figure that's their choice. If I'm not what they want, better to find out sooner rather than later. You know?"

"True. While we're on the subject... About the other day... I don't know what came over me. I've been feeling a bit over-whelmed by all the gratitude everyone keeps expressing. I don't feel like I did anything all that great."

"You mean you don't think my life is important enough. That saving me shouldn't be considered great?" Dillon, this time, feigns deep hurt.

"No, I didn't mean that."

"I know, I'm teasing you."

"I'm not sure why I reacted to that woman that way."

"As I said earlier, she's a friend of the twins since childhood. We grew up together. She's like another sister to me."

They are both quiet a few minutes. "Maybe Doc is right."

"About what?"

"Us."

"What about us?"

"Maybe we're both a bit jealous. I did some internet search-ing about the connection between 'the saved and the saver' in situations like ours. Everything says that, like it or not, a special bond is created by the experience. It says both parties just need to figure out how to deal with the emotions that come with it."

Mysti lets the boys back in. They each receive a good rustling from Dillon before going to their drying spots. Mysti puts out their food before leaving to take Dillon home.

Mysti pulls up in front of Dillon's place. "Let me walk you to the door. It's pretty icy and you don't need to slip and fall."

On the walk to his door, it is Mysti that nearly falls. Evoking a round of laughter from them both. "Maybe I'd have been better off without your help tonight," Dillon teases, reaching his door at last. "Seriously though, I want to thank you for today. I'm sure your day didn't go at all the way you had planned. I hadn't intended to take up so much of your time."

"It's all good. On the bright side, I picked up a sizeable job for Van Strien Construction, thanks to you."

"There's that. Good night, Mysti."

They stand staring at each other for long moments. Dillon feels drawn to close the mere inches between them, take her in his arms, kiss his gratitude into her. He slowly leans forward, watching the emotions play across Mysti's features.

"I need to get going," Mysti announces a single moment before their lips meet. Moving away abruptly causing Dillon to stumble slightly forward. "Goodnight, Dillon. Sweet dreams," she calls as she departs.

Sweet Dreams? Dillon's mind taunts. Ha!

"Goodnight, Mysti. Sleep well."

"Good morning, Mom, Dad," Mysti greets her parents as they enter the job site office.

"You're here early, Dear," Cora observes.

"Yeah, I didn't sleep well last night. I had ideas racing through my mind for a new project I'm going to be placing a bid on."

"What new project?" her parents speak in unison.

Mysti gives her parents the cliff notes version of yesterday's events. Clearly omitting the issues between Dillon and herself.

"So, Dillon was there with you for the day?"

"Mom, don't go trying to read things in where they aren't. Brad is his friend and doctor. He was there when he called for my assistance. That's all."

"If you say so, Dear."

"Ugh, Mom. Enough."

"Yes, Dear. Can't a mother enjoy a little fun teasing with her daughter?"

"Sorry. As I said, I didn't get much sleep. I'm a bit cranky."

"You're forgiven. I love you."

"Love you too, Mom."

"Van Strien Construction. How can I help you?" Mysti answers the office phone on Monday afternoon.

"May I speak to Mysti, please?"

"Speaking."

"Oh, hi, Mysti this is Brad Barton. I was wondering if you might be able to do the walkthrough later this afternoon or evening?"

"Hello, Dr. Barton..."

"Brad, please."

"Ok, Brad. Actually, I do have some time later today. I've had ideas running through my brain all night. "What would be a good time for you?"

"Would four o'clock work for you?"

"Sure. I'll see you at your place at four o'clock then."

"A date? With who?" Autumn asks eavesdropping.

"Not a date. A walkthrough appointment for a new project. Actually, I'd love it if you'd go along with me. This is possibly a very big project and I would appreciate extra eyes on the walk-through and some input of ideas. I barely slept last night with ideas running rampant. You could help reel me in, so I don't overwhelm this client."

"Sure. I didn't know we had a new project."

"I got it yesterday.

"Yesterday? Seriously? On Sunday of a Holiday weekend? How...?"

"Dillon called and ask for help for a friend."

"Sure, I'll go with you. Will Dillon be there?"

"No. I mean, I don't think so. What does it matter? It's not his place."

"Just wondering," Autumn says brightly. "What time today?"

"Brad said to meet him at four. We should leave here around three-thirty, three-forty?"

The Van Strien sisters ring the bell at Dr. Barton's home minutes after his arrival home.

Opening the door, "Mysti, hi. Oh, and...uh..." caught off guard by the sight of a second beautiful woman at his door, Brad stammers.

"Dr. Barton, this is my sister Autumn. Autumn, this is our potential new client, Dr. Brad Barton."

"Hello, pleasure to meet you," Brad eyes the blond haired, blue eyed version of Mysti. It strikes Brad as strange how their features could look so much alike yet be completely opposite in coloring.

"Likewise," Autumn replies staring, taking in the refined good looks of this clean-cut, dark haired, deep brown eyed man-candy before her.

"Um, come in, please. Welcome."

Mysti doesn't miss the mutual flustered flush experienced by her two companions and chuckles inwardly.

"I didn't realize you were bringing anyone with you."

"Is that a problem?"

"No. I...uh... not at all," Brad clears his throat, trying to collect himself. "Can I take your coats?"

"This is such a great house," Autumn says looking around taking in the quaint charm of the older home.

"That's exactly what I thought when I first walked in. Which is why I bought it. I love the old charm and can see the potential it has in being refurbished to maintain its quaint character, but with modern updates and amenities."

Brad sees Mysti has withdrawn some papers from her briefcase, "Shall we sit?" he motions to the dining table.

The trio sits and discusses what Mysti has already come up with, before walking through each area of the house, jotting notes of more ideas as well as issues they discover that will need to be addressed.

As the appointment is drawing to a conclusion, Autumn asks, "How is it exactly that you two met on a Sunday of a holiday weekend and ended up talking business?"

"My best friend and patient, is the guy your sister saved from freezing to death. I dropped by to see him yesterday to see if he knew anything about windows because one of mine got stuck open. He came over and gave it a try, but... I asked if he knew anyone who might know how to get it closed. He called Mysti, who promptly came to *my* rescue this time."

"We got to talking about the house while we waited for the pizza to arrive. Brad said he wants to refurbish and remodel and asked if we might be interested in the job."

"So, you two had dinner together?" Autumn asks with a hint of teasing.

"Oh, yes, well Dillon was here too. In fact, Mysti kindly drove Dillon home for me. By the way, how'd that go?"

Autumn's brows raise in question.

"It was fine."

"Just fine?" Autumn inquires.

"Yes, just fine," Mysti sounds almost indignant. "We stopped by my place to let the boys out and so Dillon could say hi to them. I drove him home and dropped him off. End of story."

Autumn knows better than to push her sister on the subject any further and lets it drop.

"Give me a couple of days to work up an in-depth bid and I'll get in touch with you to go over the details and see if you're interested in moving forward with the project."

"Sounds great. Hey, Dillon mentioned you all might be going to the Solstice Festival. When exactly is that?"

"The festival takes place on the 19th and 20th this year. Are you thinking of going too?"

"I've been giving it some thought. I've never been, even though I have a cabin up there. Are you going, too?" His question is directed to Autumn.

"Of course. Our parents bought their cabin when Harlan was five and Hugh was three. Hey, that means this is the 30th year they've all been going. Mysti and I've gone every year since we were born. It's fun. You should come along. I think Dillon's whole family is joining us this year," Autumn replies.

"I think I will. I'll talk it over with Dillon and get all the details."

"Great," Autumn smiles brightly.

"You have to promise you'll show me around and make sure I don't miss any of the good stuff. Ok?"

"Deal."

"Great. I'm looking forward to it."

Mysti and Autumn leave. "Looks like you've found a new interest," Mysti observes jokingly, enjoying seeing her little sister's rosy blush, having nothing to do with the winter wind.

Brad calls Dillon, filling him in on the afternoon's activity, telling him he's going up to the festival too. "So, what's the story with Mysti's sister? Do you know anything about her?"

"You mean like is she single?" Dillon laughs lightly.

"Well, yeah. I mean, she seems really nice and she is really cute."

"I don't know much. She didn't have anyone with her at Thanksgiving dinner, but that doesn't necessarily mean she's single. Ask Mysti next time you talk."

"Could you ask her?"

"You're the one doing business with her. I have no reason to talk to her."

"See that would give you a reason to talk to her. Call her and ask her for me."

"What, are we in middle school? Seriously? Ask Autumn yourself. Leave Mysti and me out of it."

"Fine. How'd your ride home go last night?"

Dillon hesitates to respond, unsure what Mysti may have said. Realizing she wouldn't have mentioned the awkward almost-kiss moment, "Fine."

"Just fine?" Brad responds as Autumn had to Mysti.

"Yes, just fine. We stopped by her place to let the boys out and so I could say hi to them. Then she drove me home."

"That's it?"

"Yes, That's it. End of story."

"Did you two rehearse your answers?"

"No, why?"

"Darn sure you used the exact same words Mysti did when asked the same questions. So, what really happened?"

"Nothing. Drop it."

"Ok. For now, my friend."

Mysti spends the majority of Tuesday working on the project proposal and estimated costs, compiling all the necessary data to provide Brad with the most accurate bid she can.

Wednesday Mysti calls Brad to ask if they can meet to go over the details.

"I'll be off work at six. Why don't we meet at this great little restaurant I know? It will be dinner time and we can grab a bite to eat while we go over the proposal."

"Sounds good. What's the name of the restaurant?"

"Francie's Freshly Fine Fare. Do you know it?"

Mysti smiles to herself, "Yes, it's my favorite place. I'll meet you there around six thirty?"

"Perfect. See you then."

"Hey, Dillon. What are you up to?"

"Not much. Writing. Trying to obey my doctor's orders and stay off my leg. Why? What are you up to?"

"I was just wondering if you'd like to get out of the house for a bit and join me for dinner tonight. I'll pick you up at six. We'll go to that place we love, Francie's Freshly Fine Fare."

"Yeah, I suppose I could take a break for a while. Save me from eating cereal again for dinner."

"Yes, your doctor says you need better nutrition. I'll see you later."

Brad arrives to pick Dillon up. "Ready? Let's go." Brad is hoping to be seated before Mysti arrives, so she doesn't see Dillon right away.

Brad approaches the hostess with his back to Dillon. A finger to his lips in shushing fashion, he whispers, "Table for three. A young lady will be arriving looking to be seated with Dr. Brad

Barton. Without letting on there is another person with me, please bring her to my table," he hands her a twenty.

"There's no need for that, Sir. I'll see to it."

"I know you will. This is a token of appreciation."

She takes them to a four-top table.

"Hey, Suzy. You're working late. Why are you still here?'"

"Working a double. The night hostess called in sick. What are you doing here this late? You usually only come get lunch."

"I'm meeting a prospective client to go over the bid."

"Oh, Dr. Barton?"

"Yes."

"He said someone was meeting him. He didn't say who. Right this way."

Suzy leads Mysti to the table. Brad sees her coming and rises to greet her. Dillon looks up at Brad curiously.

"Hello, Brad."

"Good evening. Glad you made it."

Mysti shakes Brad's hand. It registers that Dillon is seated at the table.

"What's going on?" Dillon asks Brad as Brad pulls out the chair next to Dillon guiding Mysti to take a seat.

"That's what I was about to ask. What's he doing here?"

"Oh, did I *forget* to mention to either of you the other would be here? Oops, my bad. I'm sorry." Brad smiles broadly.

"No, you're not," Dillon and Mysti speak in unison, causing Brad to laugh.

"Look, Dillon. You're my best friend and I wanted you with me to go over the proposal and bid Mysti is here to present. For some reason, I just knew that neither of you would have agreed to this meeting if you knew the other was going to be here. I don't know what's up with that, but that's for you two to figure out, sooner rather than later. Tonight, you're both here for me. Got it?"

Dillon and Mysti look at each other. "Fine," they sigh in unison.

"Good."

The server takes their orders. Mysti makes a mental note that both men order vegetarian, which she has a feeling is in deference to her.

They go over the documents Mysti has prepared while waiting for their food and while they eat. Talking animatedly about the vision for the project. They all seem in full agreement.

"When do you think you'd like to get started with phase one?"

"Right after the first of the year, if that's possible for your company's schedule."

"I'm sure we can work it in. I'll talk it over with my dad and let you know sometime next week."

"Or you can just let me know at the festival."

"That's right. We'll be seeing you there in a couple of weeks. Looks like we may end up with the largest contingent attending en masse, the festival has ever seen."

"How many are going?"

"At last check..." Mysti pauses to count in her head, "22 including you."

"Wow. As an only child, I come from a very small family, this is going to be some experience."

As they leave, Brad says to Mysti with a wink, "I won't ask you to drive my pal home tonight."

"Thanks. Saves me from saying no," she responds also with a wink.

"Geeze. I didn't realize I'm such an imposition," Dillon sounds truly hurt this time.

"Nah. We still love ya bro." Brad assures him with a shoulder hug.

Both Mysti and Dillon register Brad's use of *we* in his profession of love.

Dillon asks the age-old question, "*We?* Do you have a mouse in your pocket?"

"Of course not. *We* as in Mysti and me. Right Mysti?" Brad responds, now giving Mysti a shoulder hug. Then laughs heartily at the expressions playing across both their faces. "See you soon, Mysti. Drive safe." Brad steers Dillon out the door.

"Hey, brother. Tyce and I have a party to go to Friday night and Dathan and Danna are having a holiday party for their friends at their house. Can we count on you to babysit all the kids for us? We'll bring them to you. It will be easier that way."

"Of course. Have I ever turned down spending time with the kids?"

"No. Just want to be sure you're up to it."

"We'll have a blast like we always do. What time?

The kids all get dropped off around four so the adults have plenty of time to get ready for their respective events and the kids have plenty of time to hang with their uncle.

A couple hours after their arrival, dinner eaten and more fun begun, Bridgit gets the other kids to keep Uncle Dillon occupied while she sneaks Dillon's phone and finds Mysti's number and secretly calls her.

"Hello?"

"Hi, Mysti?"

"Yes."

"This is Bridgit, Dillon's niece."

"Hi, Bridgit. What's up? Is everything OK?"

"Well, yes and no. I mean, us kids, all of us, are at Uncle Dillon's and well I need your help."

"Where are your parents and grandparents?"

"They're at Christmas parties and we don't want to disturb them so I thought maybe you could come over and help."

"Is someone hurt?"

"No, it's well, I don't know how to explain, I just need you to come over. Please?"

"Where's Dillon?"

"He's handling the boys, and well this is more of a girl thing."

Mysti sighs deeply not sure what to make of this, but she hears a kind of pleading in this young girl's voice and figures maybe she can be of help. Maybe it's a female issue she doesn't feel comfortable telling her uncle.

"Ok, Sweetie. I'll come over. I'll be there shortly."

Bridgit gives covert thumbs-up to the other kids when she returns to the dining room where they are at the table playing a board game with Uncle Dillon.

Mysti rings the bell.

"Who could that be?" Dillon asks no one in particular.

"I'll get it," Bridgit announces, rushing to the door.

"Hi, Bridgit. Everything OK?"

"Better now. Come on in. Let me take your coat."

"Bridgit, who is it?" Dillon asks as he steps into the living room to investigate.

"Mysti? Hi. What are you doing here?" Dillon asks perplexed.

"Hi. Uh, well Bridgit called me and said she needed me and asked me to come over," she explains while giving him a look that she hopes he'll understand, "She said it is more of a girl thing? Said all the parents and grandparents are at parties and she doesn't want to disturb them."

Dillon catches on to what she is alluding to. "Oh, uh yes. Well, that is really sweet of you to come to help.

Bridgit catches on that her ploy worked. Now is the time to let on what 'help' is needed.

The other kids come out now, "Hi, Mysti." they all call out running to hug her. "We're glad you could come to help us."

Dillon and Mysti look at each other, now both confused. Mysti, eyebrows drawn together in a near scowl, looks at Bridgit, "I thought...?"

"Care to explain, Bridgit my dear?" Dillon asks holding back obvious upset.

"Well, we wanted to bake Christmas cookies and we know you don't bake very good, 'cause it's more of a girl thing, so I decided to call and ask Mysti to help."

Mysti closes her eyes, inhaling deeply shaking her head.

Dillon's brows raise, "More of a girl thing. That's what you told Mysti? You tricked Mysti into coming here, thinking *you specifically* needed girl issue help?"

"Well, I just said it was more of a girl thing because baking is more of a girl thing," Bridgit looks coyly at her uncle playing the sweet innocent niece card.

Mysti watches the array of emotions play across Dillon's features. He looks at the other four children who also, right on cue, grace their uncle with angelic smiles of hope.

"Please?" Parker pleads

"Pretty please?" Brooke begs.

"Please, Uncle?" Elton and Elias request.

Dillon looks at Mysti, both suddenly fighting back smiles. Dillon covers his face with both hands, shaking his head, saying as he lowers his hands, "I cannot believe the devious deception displayed by the five of you tonight."

Mysti hears a tone of anger seep into his next words.

"I can't believe my nieces and nephews would intentionally prey on the kindness of anyone, let alone Mysti, by leading her to think that someone needed real help. Knowing her wonderful kind heart wouldn't allow her to say no."

"Dillon, it's ok. There's no need to be angry with them," Mysti tries to calm him as she sees the regret and sadness well up in all five children's expressions.

"It's not ok."

"Yes, it is this time."

Mysti gathers all five children in front of her and squats down to their eye level. "Do all of you understand what part of this is wrong?" she looks at each.

"Kind of," Elton responds.

"Have any of you heard the story of 'The Boy Who Cried Wolf'?"

"No," they all respond.

"Well, the short version is that a little boy cried 'Wolf!' causing the adults to come running to save him even though there wasn't a wolf. He did it so many times that one day there really was a wolf and he cried for help and everyone ignored him and he got hurt by the wolf. Which just means, don't pretend to need help if you don't really need it because then one day if you really need help you might not get it. Do you understand?"

All five nod their heads sheepishly.

"OK. We will use this incident today as a lesson. Uncle Dillon? Do you have baking supplies to bake Christmas cookies?"

"Truthfully? Probably not."

"Fine, then Bridgit and Elton will go with me to the store to get supplies while you four, clear up the kitchen and dining area, preheat the oven, get out bowls, measuring cups, measure spoons, mixing spoons and cookie sheets."

"Mysti, you don't have to do this. We shouldn't reward their deceitfulness."

Mysti again gets the attention of all five kids, "Here's the deal. Everyone, place your right hand on your uncle Dillon and repeat after me."

The kids all do as told.

"I... state your name..."

They each input their name. "I..."

"Do solemnly swear on the life of Uncle Dillon,"

"Do solemnly swear on the life of Uncle Dillon,"

"that from this day forward,"

"that from this day forward,"

"I will not be devious and deceitful."

"I will not be devious and deceitful."

"I will be on my best behavior,"

"I will be on my best behavior,"

"and we will donate half of all cookies baked this night,"

"and we will donate half of all cookies baked this night,"

"to those less fortunate than myself."

"to those less fortunate than myself."

"Ok, the clock is ticking. Get busy," Mysti instructs Dillon plus three. "Get your coats, let's go," she directs the other two.

Mysti, Bridgit and Elton return with bags and bags of supplies. She even buys a couple of cookie sheets as she figures Dillon, being a bachelor and not having baking supplies, probably doesn't have one. She is correct.

Dillon turns on Christmas music. They look up delicious sugar cookie and gingerbread cookie recipes and get to work baking and decorating dozens and dozens of cookies.

The mixing station is set up at the kitchen counter, the decorating station is on the dining table. Mysti and Dillon stand side by side assisting, coaching and working along with the kids.

Dillon, standing near Mysti, pauses, looking into her eyes, seeing the joy flashing there from within.

Mysti returns the eye contact, seeing puzzlement and happiness exuding from within.

Bridgit sees the two adults gazing into each other's eyes, nudging Elton, nodding Mysti and Uncle Dillon's direction. Bridgit and Elton smile brightly, low-fiving, out of sight of the adults. The kids watch as Dillon whispers, "Thank you."

To which Mysti whispers her reply, "My pleasure."

There is flour, powdered sugar and pretty much every baking ingredient everywhere, including on everyone. They sing joyfully along with the festive songs playing loudly.

At the end of a song Bridgit tells Mysti, "That is one of the songs the school choir, all five of us are in, will be singing at our concert on the sixteenth."

"Will you come to our concert?" Elton asks, excited hopefulness in his voice.

"Please? And we have a dance recital next Saturday the twelfth. You just *have* to come to that. All of us kids will be dancing in that too."

"Yea! You have to come. Please?"

"Please?"

"Pleeeease?" They all begin to beg.

"Guys!" Dillon interrupts loudly over their pleading. "If you intend to ask Mysti to attend, that's fine, although you have to remember she has her own life, but don't beg and plead. Ask in a polite, respectful manner and graciously accept whatever the answer is. Got It?"

"Yes, Uncle Dillon," five sad little voices respond.

"I tell you what, you send me the information for both events and I will see if I can work either or both into my schedule. OK?"

"Hurrah."

"Cool."

"Yippee."

"Yay."

"Agreed, but how will I get the information to you?" Bridgit asks.

"I'll give you, my number. You can text it to me since you obviously know how to use a cell phone," Mysti concludes in a teasing tone with a wink.

They all return to their boisterous singing, laughing and exuberant talking. They are so loud that no one hears the front door open nor sees the four adults enter. The undetected observers all pull out cell phones and begin video recording and taking photos of the jubilant chaos taking place. After a few minutes, the parents make their presence known by joining in on the fun, starting by joining the singing.

Eventually, the energy level begins to wind down as they finish up the last of the decorating and boxing up of the finished products.

"What brought this about?" Devan asks as everyone pitches in to clean up.

Dillon and Mysti smirk and look at Bridgit who sheepishly admits, "It was my idea. I got the other kids to play along to get Mysti here," Bridgit sobers, "I'm sorry Mom and Dad. I was deceitful. I tricked Mysti into coming over."

Surprised expressions overtake all four parents.

Dillon interjects, "But Mysti forgave them and she extracted a solemn oath from them all that they will never be deceitful or devious again. She even made them vow it on my life."

"Well, that ought to make them keep their promise," Tyce asserts.

"Dare I ask what prompted you kids to coerce Mysti over here?" Dathan inquires.

"We had so much fun with Mysti on Thanksgiving and she and Uncle Dillon are both alone. Brooke and I heard Grandma say Uncle Dillon sounded happy when he was stuck with Mysti, but he seems sad since he came home. We kids talked it over and decided Uncle Dillon needed to spend some time with Mysti again so he can be happy again."

"From what I saw when we walked in here tonight, you kids were spot on," Danna attests.

Dillon's and Mysti's eyes meet. Dillon's glisten with the moisture his niece's words evoked.

Mysti's eyes cloud over trying to hide the emotions racing within her. "Glad to have been of service... again. You go see your family off. I'll finish up the cleaning then I'll get going."

Mysti returns to the kitchen. Devan follows her indicating to the others to collect the children and their belongings to head home.

"Mysti?"

"Yes."

"It appears you misunderstood. The kids didn't get you here to provide a service for making Dillon happy. They concocted a plan to get you here so you and Dillon could be happy together and like Danna said, it worked. I have proof."

Devan plays back the video she took when they arrived. The video shows Dillon and Mysti surrounded by five little ones. Dillon and Mysti singing a Christmas carol in harmony, looking at each other with hearts overflowing with joy.

Mysti's eyes overflow and she turns away. Devan steps to her, turning Mysti and wrapping her arms around her. Bridgit comes into the room, she also wraps her arms around Mysti. "I'm sorry Mysti. I didn't mean to upset you," Bridgit chokes out past her tears.

Mysti takes Bridgit in her arms, "You didn't upset me. You gave me a most glorious gift tonight - a priceless gift. A gift that can never be bought, returned, replaced or taken away. The gift of joy and time spent with and loving you kids. The gift of eternally memorable moments."

Bridgit looks Mysti in the eye, "But being with Uncle Dillon didn't make you happy? Don't you like him?"

"Yes, sweetie. I was happy to spend time with your uncle. Of course, I like him. He's a very nice man and an amazing Uncle. Thank you for having me come tonight so that he could have fun and be happy. Now you need to get home to bed and I need to finish cleaning up so that your uncle doesn't have to wake up to our disaster zone. OK?"

Bridgit nods and hugs Mysti sincerely. "I love you Bridgit," Mysti states truthfully. "Sleep well."

Mysti stands at the kitchen sink washing the final few dishes. The music has been turned down to a soft ambient level, the families have departed. Dillon hobbles into the kitchen to stand behind Mysti. He whispers near her ear, a gentle teasing to his tone, "Aha, I've got you now and the bears aren't here to save you."

Mysti becomes nervous. This is actually the first time other than while driving him home that she has been completely alone with Dillon.

Dillon feels her energy level instantly shoot from relaxed to tense. He takes a half step back. That was not the reaction he had hoped for. What had he hoped for? He asks himself.

"Mysti, please relax. I'm not going to hurt you. I'm only joking," he lays a hand on her shoulder. Every muscle in her tightens in reaction. Dillon steps away. "Ok. Giving you space."

"I'm sorry. I...just. I mean, I know you wouldn't intentionally hurt me. I'm just scared."

"Of what? Surely not me?"

"Not specifically you, but of me and indirectly you, yes. I can't explain. I just need to get this finished and get home."

"I'll finish up. You can go home now. I don't want to keep you. I mean I never intended this evening to go this way as I'm sure you didn't either. I'm sorry my niece dragged you out of the comfort of your home and into this chaos. I understand she meant well, but this wasn't fair to you. You've already done so much."

"I enjoyed the evening. I had a very good time. You have wonderful nieces and nephews. As you know, we don't have any youngsters around. I thoroughly enjoyed myself." Mysti continues washing as she speaks and finishes. "That's the last dish. I'll be leaving now. Thank you for allowing me to participate in this activity with the kids. Good night," she retrieves her jacket as she spiels off her parting words.

Dillon stands watching Mysti, somewhat dumbfounded. She seems so very different from the woman he's just spent hours baking cookies with, singing; laughing. He tries to replay all that happened since the arrival of his siblings and pinpoint the moment the switch was flipped that changed her.

Mysti steps out the door of Dillon's condo, "Goodnight, Mysti. Drive safely, please. Sweet dreams."

"Thanks, sleep well."

The following morning Mysti receives a text from a number she doesn't recognize.

"Hi, Mysti. This is Bridgit texting from my mom's phone. Yes, I have permission. Here are the details for both events we talked about last night. We all reeeally hope you can come to both events. It would be great to have you there, but as Uncle Dillon said last night, we know you have your own life and we will understand if you are not able to make it. Thank you again for last night. We all had so much fun. Hope you had fun too. Hugs, Bridgit."

There are photo attachments of two invitations for the two events.

Mysti responds simply, "I'll think about it."

"Hello, Harlan," Mysti answers a Sunday morning call.

"Hey, little sis. What are your plans for today?"

"Writing. Why what's up?"

"Well, I thought maybe you'd be willing to go with me to help me pick out a tree for my place."

"You know how I feel about cut trees. That's why I have an artificial tree."

"Yes, I know and I'm right there with you. That's why I found this cool tree place that only sells Living Trees. Thought maybe you might want to get one, too."

"Really? OK, I'll go with you. What time?"

"As soon as you're ready. Say, an hour? I'll pick you up."

"OK, see you then."

"Polar, Grizzly, Kodiak. Come eat, boys," Mysti feeds the boys then lets them back out in the six-foot-high fenced backyard to enjoy the sunny day lying around in the snow while she goes tree shopping with Harlan.

"Good morning, Kiersten," Dillon greets upon answering his phone.

"Morning big brother. What do you have planned for your day?"

"Oh, you know. A little skiing, maybe a long hike and a quick 5k run. Why what's up with you?"

"Ha-ha, very funny. I thought you might be feeling a bit bored and cooped up and since you are supposed to be doing some walking to exercise your leg, I thought maybe you'd want to go with me to get a tree for the apartment."

"You know how I feel about cut trees."

"Exactly. That's the reason I thought you might enjoy this. I found a cool tree place that only sells Living Trees. Thought maybe I could even talk you into a small one for your place."

"I don't know..."

"Please? It will do you good to get a little fresh air. The sun is shining, the temps are warm, it's a beautiful day."

"OK, I'll go. The best reason though is so I can spend some time with you."

"Yay. I'll pick you up in an hour. Love you, big brother."

"Love you too little sis."

"This is such a great idea. This is the perfect solution for people that want real trees with the benefit of not participating in the mass killing of hundreds of thousands of innocent trees every year." Mysti is so glad Harlan brought her to this eco-friendly tree farm. "How much do these trees cost?" Mysti asks the attendant.

"I was just about to ask the same question," Kiersten pipes up.

"Kiersten? Hi, fancy meeting you here," Mysti greets Dillon's sister.

"You here alone?" they ask in unison, then laugh.

Mysti answers first. "No, my brother Harlan asked me to come help him pick out a tree."

"How funny. I asked my brother to come help me pick out a tree. I know he doesn't like cut trees..."

"Me either."

"I heard about this place and thought this would be a chance for him to get out for a bit and maybe get a tree for his place too." With that Dillon and Harlan approach from a few rows over.

"Look who I found," Harlan announces just before realizing Kiersten is standing there with Mysti. Four adolescent-esque hellos are sheepishly uttered.

Mysti recovers first. "I'm sorry," she speaks to the attendant, "as I was asking, what is the pricing for your trees?"

"We have two options."

The other three members of the group now tune it to hear also, "Our trees can either be purchased or rented. Or as I like to refer to it, *adopted* to a forever home or *fostered* for the season," the attendant states.

"Rented?" Harlan inquires.

"Yes, since the main objective of Living Trees is to not kill them, and because not everyone has the ability keep the potted trees or a location to plant their living tree after the holidays we have the rental option. Meaning that you purchase the tree at cost, then after the holidays are over, you bring the tree back to us and receive a refund of 50% of the purchase price. Then we tend to the tree for the next year and sell or re-rent it. If you purchase it outright, we ask that you either transplant it into a larger pot and keep it living for future years or plant it in your or someone else's yard or somewhere out in nature so it may continue to live."

"Wow. This is an amazing idea," Harlan states.

"I can get behind this all the way," Kiersten announces.

"Why didn't anyone think of this before. I think I'll get one for my place," Mysti decides.

"I believe you've just gained four new clients and probably many more once we spread the word," Dillon tells the attendant.

"Great. Feel free to look around and pick out your 'tree children' for this year. Let me know when you're ready to sign up to adopt or foster one of our baby trees and we'll get you loaded up. If you have any other questions, don't hesitate to ask," the attendant smiles walking off to assist other clients.

"How cool is this and, by the way, how coincidentally strange and cool is it running into the two of you here?" Harlan asks, smiling brightly at Kiersten, which, doesn't go unnoticed by either Mysti or Dillon, who try to cover their amused smirks at the obvious attraction between their siblings.

However, the sight of Dillon's sparkling eyes ignites a warming sensation that creeps under Mysti's skin and causes her breath to catch. She glances away coyly as Dillon inhales sharply, clears his throat announcing, "Hey, little sis, shall we get to picking out our trees?"

The tension between Dillon and Mysti doesn't go unnoticed by either Harlan or Kiersten, who both half-successfully hold back their own smirks. They all look at each other and in near unison ask. "What?" then all chuckle as they begin to wander, looking at trees of various sizes.

Somehow Mysti and Kiersten end up meandering together. Harlan and Dillon do also.

"You know, I'm going to call my parents and tell them about this place," Dillon states, pulling out his phone.

"That's a great idea. I'm calling my parents and siblings too," Harlan agrees.

A few minutes later the foursome meets back up. "You know, in so many of the Christmas movies they show families carrying on the tradition of buying pre-cut or cutting down their Christmas tree together and it has always annoyed me that the killing of trees is a perpetuated tradition. This? Coming as a family, or part of a family in this case, and choosing a tree to share the holiday, knowing that the next year the tree gets to share Christmas with another family and the tree will live on? This is a tradition I can get behind wholeheartedly," Mysti informs the others.

Harlan tells Mysti, "I called Mom and she is going to call the rest of the family and tell them to come here too."

Harlan takes a stance with fists on hips and speaks in a tone like the Viking he resembles, "I hereby proclaim today the beginning of a new Van Strien family tradition. Hear! Hear!"

Kiersten, Dillon and Mysti chuckle slightly as they join in and all cheer, "Hear! Hear!"

Kiersten looks to Dillon almost questioningly, "Yes, I too called Mom and she also intends to let the family know to start coming here."

"I hereby proclaim today the beginning of a new Lubbers family tradition. Hear! Hear!" Harlan repeats the proclamation.

Kiersten, Dillon and Mysti chuckle again as they repeat their previous cheer, "Hear! Hear!"

The attendant comes over to check on their progress. "Yes, I believe we have each picked out a tree." They go about getting their trees. Mysti observes the farms system and a thought comes to her which she shares with the attendant, "I see you have metal tags wired to each tree with tracking numbers to verify the tree being returned is one of yours. Is that correct?"

"Yes."

"I was just thinking that with all our modern technology I wonder if there might be a way to *chip* the trunk of each tree like people chip their pets. That way maybe there'd be less chance of the tag falling off and getting lost. Then you could scan the tree into a database that would keep track of information. For instance; when the tree was planted, each time the tree is fostered, the family names of who fosters it, when it's returned, it's height each year to watch its growth. Maybe have a sight that people could go to when they foster a tree to see the information.

Where they could post pictures of how the tree is decorated at their home and tell a short story of the tree's experience with their family. Kind of like the tree's life story, so people can feel part of the tree's history. Maybe it's a crazy idea but..."

"Not crazy at all. I think it is an awesome idea. Do you mind if I tell my parents? They own the farm. I think they'd love the idea and would look into trying to do that."

"Of course, I don't mind you telling them. I hope they do like the idea and are able to implement it."

The others have been listening in and all agree it is a great idea. Then as if two minds hopped into the same vehicle at once, headed in the same direction, it appears Dillon and Mysti have the same question and idea and begin to speak together, "What will you do..." they begin. "Go ahead, it's your turn to ask your question," Mysti offers.

"What will you do when the trees become too large to foster to homes?"

"I don't think Mom and Dad have thought that far ahead yet."

"Our family business is a landscaping company. We often have clients who wish to have more mature trees for their landscaping vision. They are so expensive and difficult to find, maybe we could work out a deal that when trees become too large to be household Christmas trees, we could possibly adopt them for a bit less than the nurseryies' outrageous purchase prices and give them forever homes in someone's landscape design."

"Wow! That sounds amazing to me and I would bet my parents would love the idea. You all are such great people with such great ideas. I am so glad you came here today."

"Thank you. What was it you were going to say?" Dillon asks Mysti.

"Basically the same thing actually. Our family business is residential and commercial construction. We often have clients who are interested in having mature landscaping and ask if we know where to get mature trees for less. I was going to say we could tell them to check with you, but that might be more than your parents want to deal with so we could get them in contact with his company and they could handle it."

"That sounds perfect."

Before leaving, Dillon and Mysti give the attendant their business cards to give the owners. "It has been an absolute pleasure coming here and meeting you today. I look forward to many years to come of our new tradition," Mysti tells the attendant.

The Van Striens and Lubbers make their way to their vehicles to depart.

Harlan seemingly not ready to end their time together asks, "Would the two of you like to join Mysti and I for lunch? My treat."

Mysti shoots her brother a quizzical look as if to say, *'who said anything about lunch? I'm supposed to be home writing.'*

Kiersten answers, "Sure, that sounds great. I'm starved."

Dillon shoots his sister a quizzical look as if to say, *'who said anything about lunch? I'm supposed to be home writing.'*

Mysti and Dillon look at each other acknowledging their siblings have a thing for each other and they are being caught up in the attempts to prolong this outing. Both roll their eyes in acceptance and go along with the plan, neither wanting to be the one to put a kink in the siblings' romantic chances.

Besides, Dillon admits to himself, he isn't interested in this outing ending just yet either.

Besides, Mysti admits to herself, she isn't interested in this outing ending just yet either.

At lunch, talk covers many topics from the morning's activities to the possibilities they'd broached about the future of the mature trees to the upcoming festival. The conversation comes 'round to the decorating of their individual trees.

Harlan, always a bit competitive and adept at working things to get what he wants, "Hey, why don't we have a team tree decorating challenge?"

"What do you have in mind?" Dillon asks hesitant, but curious. "Family against family?"

"I thought you and Mysti against Kiersten and me. Then we can get the families to vote to see who wins."

Kiersten winks at Mysti, "Why not have Mysti and me against you two?" she asks teasing in her tone.

"No way. That wouldn't be fair or fun," Harlan asserts.

"We could do it that you guys could do one tree together and we girls could do one together then we could do the other two trees in the teams you suggested," Mysti suggests.

"That sounds good to me," Harlan responds.

"Deal," Dillon agrees.

"What are the prizes we are competing for?" Kiersten inquires.

Everyone thinks...

Kiersten offers, "In the girls against guys, the losers cook a homemade dinner for the winners."

"Deal," they all concur.

"In the couples' challenge, losers treat winners to a couples spa day," Harlan suggests.

"You do know that we're not *couples*, right?" Mysti asks her brother.

"You know what I mean. One guy and one girl teams."

"But a couples spa day is indicative of actual couples. I'm not sure I'd want to win that."

"See, you don't have to worry about that since you won't be winning. You'll be paying for us to go," Harlan puts an arm around Kiersten's shoulder, bringing a blush to her face.

"We'll see about that," Dillon replies, taking Mysti's hand in his, catching her off guard she nearly jerks it away, but he holds tight.

Dillon releases her hand to shake on the deal with Harlan and Kiersten. Mysti isn't sure if she's glad or sad the contact ends so quickly. Mysti also shakes on the deal with the other two.

Over the remainder of lunch, the pairings make arrangements to get in touch to plan and execute their décor. Lunch officially over, the four make their way to the parking lot to say their goodbyes. Harlan takes Mysti home and takes her tree in then visits with the bears, romping in the yard with them a while before heading home.

Kiersten takes Dillon home. She takes his tree in the condo for him.

"I take it you've taken a liking to Harlan."

"What? I don't know what you're talking about," Kiersten plays coy with her brother.

"You know exactly what I'm talking about."

"No more so than you have taken a liking to Mysti," Kiersten retorts.

"What? I don't know what *you're* talking about," Dillon tries to sound convincing.

"You see that Harlan and I like each other and I see that you and Mysti like each other. The difference is, Harlan and I aren't trying to fool ourselves and others by trying to pretend we don't. Unlike the two of you are trying to do and, by the way, you're both failing miserably. Later big brother," Kiersten hugs her brother goodbye. "I don't understand why you both seem so averse to liking each other, but you should both get over it and see where it goes."

"You do know my reason."

"Not everyone is like Carla."

"Maybe not, but I'm not ready to take that chance."

"Seriously? You're going to let some psycho woman from your past dictate your future? You're seriously going to give Carla that much power over your life? Where's the strong-willed, independent, take no crap, big brother I have worshiped my whole life?" Kiersten looks skyward calling out, "Hey, aliens who abducted my big brother, I demand you bring him back, now! Because this man before me, willing to allow some psychotic woman's bad behavior dictate and control his future, is *not* My brother. I will not accept this imposter. You hear me?" She turns back to Dillon, "You hear me?" she looks him straight in the eye. They stand long moments in a stare-down of sorts.

Taking his little sister in his arms, "Yes, Kiersten. I hear you. You're right. When did you grow up and get so smart?"

I learned from my older siblings, you in particular. I love you, Dillon. I won't, and you can't, let Carla ruin your life. You deserve to love, really love and be truly loved in return. I don't know if that's meant to be with Mysti for sure, but you'll never know if you don't let go of the past and open up to the possibility of a future that she might be. No one in the family ever truly like Carla. Everyone truly loves Mysti. Don't forget, if not for Mysti..."

"I know! I think about that every day. I don't want to push myself on her just because I feel indebted to her for my life. I don't want to pressure her into anything. I mean I'm just some man who intruded in on her life. Turning it topsy-turvy. You don't know what she's been through so you don't understand. I don't think she has any interest in me or any man for that matter. I don't know all the details, but she lost someone she loved very much then she too was stalked more recently. I don't' want to be just another issue she has to deal with and get over."

"OK. I hear you, Dillon. I'll back off and tell the others to also. You're right. Your appearance in her life has altered it in so many ways already. Maybe it is a bit of overload, but from the viewpoint of the women in this family and I believe hers too, we see the joy in her when you're together just like we all see in you too." One last hug and kiss goodbye, and Kiersten leaves Dillon to ponder all that has taken place today as well as all she has just said.

The next day a variety of calls are made between the tree decorating foursome to schedule decorating times during that week for each of the four trees. They discuss who the judges should be. They all agree on four things; the judges can't know which teams decorated which trees. That the two sets of parents would probably be the most honest and unbiased simply out of fairness and that all trees must be completed for judging to take place next Sunday.

~ 6 ~

"Hey, Danna."

"Hi, Devan."

"Make sure you have all your costumes and shoes, so I don't have to run back out for anything," Devan instructs her kids as they get out of the SUV.

"Exactly. What your aunt told your cousins, same goes for you two," Danna calls to her boys over the commotion of five exuberant kids grabbing duffle bags of dance attire before heading into the Showstoppers Dance Studio.

Both Danna and Devan are very active dance moms and generally stay during practices to help in any manner necessary since all five kids dance. Today is no exception as the studio's Christmas Dance Extravaganza is this coming Saturday. They both join with other moms to put finishing touches on props, sets, costumes, banners, whatever is needed.

Sitting together gluing thousands of Swarovski Crystals on dozens of costumes, "What's your take on the deception the kids pulled on Mysti on Friday?" Danna asks.

"On one hand, I was a bit angry with Bridgit for her devious plotting, but on the other hand I was kind of proud of their imaginative well thought out plan which they implemented perfectly."

"And quite successfully. I asked Elton why they did it and he told me that they all really like Mysti and that they think Uncle Dillon needs someone to Love."

"That's what Bridgit said. She also said they think Mysti was guided to not only save Dillon from dying that night, but also to save him from being alone. When did our kids get so grown up to be thinking like that?"

"I know, right? Parker said he thinks Uncle Dillon looks happier than he has ever seen him when Mysti is around. He's only six and he has noticed that?"

"The thing is, he's right. What we witnessed the other night was so special. Like a scene from a romantic movie."

"Mom?"

"What's up, Brooke?"

"Can we invite Mysti to our dance extravaganza?"

Devan and Danna smile at one another. "I thought Bridgit already sent a text to ask her."

"She did, but Mysti said she'll think about it. We want to ask her again to make sure she remembers to think about it... and say yes."

"Ok, you can try once more on two conditions. One that you can't be upset if she is busy and unable to make it. Two this is the last time any of you ask. You will not pester Mysti."

"Yay!" Brooke rushes back to the other kids. "My mom said we can ask Mysti again," the five grab hands, jumping around cheering.

Devan and Danna chuckle, "I think we have a bunch of matchmakers on our hands."

Bridgit hurries over to her mother, "Can I borrow your phone to call Mysti and invite her again?"

"Did you save her number in my phone.?

"Yes. Besides, I memorized it when I called her from Uncle Dillon's phone the other night. How do you think I knew it to send her the text?"

"Of course, you did," Danna comments trying hard to contain her giggle.

Devan sighs as she hands over the phone.

"Guys come here!" Bridgit calls to her siblings and cousins. "Come help me invite her."

The others run over, filled with glee, while Bridgit dials Mysti's number, putting the phone on speaker.

Mysti is just finishing up work for the day at the site office when her phone rings. The caller ID displays a number she doesn't recognize and she hesitates to answer, thinking it is probably work related. She's really hungry and wants to go home to eat, but business is business. She decides to answer in the manner she always does during business hours, "Van Strien Construction, Mysti speaking. How can I help you?"

"Hi. Mysti?" Mysti recognizes the youthful female voice.

"Yes, this is Mysti. Is this Bridgit?"

"Yes."

Mysti hears the other kids saying things like, "Ask her." "Hi, Mysti." "I hope she says yes."

"Shhh!" Bridgit tells the others then speaks to Mysti, "Us kids want to remind you of our Dance Extravaganza this Saturday. All five of us will be dancing and we would really love it if you could come watch us. It would make us all so happy for you to be there. Can you come? I sent you the information. It starts at two and is supposed to end at five. I know it's kind of long, but we have a lot of dancers and a lot of special dances for this show," the question and information tumble from Bridgit.

"Wow, that's great. Um..."

"Pleeese come?" Brooke pleads

"It's going to be a great show. You'll love it." Elton informs.

"Please, Miss Mysti? I get to do my first ever tap solo. I want you to be there to see it." Parker tells Mysti.

"Wow, a solo? I take it that you have me on speaker so all of you can hear me, right? Here's the thing guys. I would absolutely love to attend your dance performance..." Five children cheer before Mysti can finish, "WAIT! Wait, wait!" Mysti calls out. The children quiet. "However, first, I hope you all aren't breaking the solemn promise you made the other night that you would never again be deceitful. Second, as much as all of you would love to have me there and as much as I'd love to be there, I'm not so sure everyone else would be as happy to have me there."

Devan and Danna have been letting the kids do this, but now intervene, "Hey, Mysti this is Devan."

"And Danna."

"We're here with our kiddos. They actually asked permission to call you this time."

"To your point. Everyone would love to have you attend."

"Oh, hi ladies. I was concerned they were going rogue again."

"Nope. My kids told me of the vow you made them swear on their uncle's life. Trust me, I don't think any of them will ever be deceitful again. They love their uncle too much to risk his life." Danna informs Mysti.

Hands clasped in a pleading manner, the kids quietly prance in place, whispering their pleas for Mysti to say she'll come.

"If you ladies are sure it will be ok for me to attend, I will."

Five screeching children jump, bounce and squeal with delight. Bridgit hands the phone to her mother.

"I'm sure you can hear how delighted the kids are."

"See you all on Saturday. Bye."

"Bye."

"Goodbye."

"Well, boys, how do I look?" Mysti asks the three bears. "I'm going for festive, but not over the top. Nice, but not too dressy. Warm, but with peel-able layers in case it is too warm in the auditorium. Comfortable, but not too casual. Did I pull it off?"

The three breathing fur rugs sigh heavily as they adjust lying positions. "Great help you guys are. Here goes nothing."

Mysti decides not to arrive early, hoping the Lubbers family will all be in and seated so she can merely slip in unnoticed and sit alone near the rear. She doesn't want to intrude on their family.

Mysti stands allowing her eyes to adjust from the sunlit, sparkling diamond-crusted, pristinely white, snow-blanketed landscape she'd driven through to the subdued, ambient lighting of the auditorium interior.

"One as radiant as you will never successfully blend in as a wallflower," proclaims the deep-timbered voice so close to Mysti's ear that she feels the warmth of the breath that carries the words to her.

Mysti feels her own breath catch as chills wash over her immediately followed by a wave of warmth. She dares not turn to respond as the nearness of the speaker is such, that she is sure such an action would bring them quite literally face to face.

Dillon gently places his hand on the small of Mysti's back, causing a flash of warmth to flare on her flesh there. "This way to your seat, milady," Dillon feigns a British accent.

"Oh, no, that's okay. I'll find a seat back here somewhere. I don't want to impose."

Dillon repositions to look Mysti in the eyes, "My family sent me to find you. They are saving you a seat. The kids will be looking for you to be there. Do you wish to disappoint them all?"

"Oh, ah, no. I don't want to disappoint anyone, though I also don't want to obtrude upon your family time."

Dillon inhales deeply, as he applies a bit of pressure at the point of contact as he gently begins to maneuver Mysti forward through the crowded aisles. "My family is awaiting your arrival. Preferably before the performances begin."

Mysti allows Dillon to guide her toward the front, where indeed his family awaits. She makes a mental note that Dillon is using a cane and isn't wearing a straight leg brace. Almost as if reading her thoughts, "I've graduated to a hinged knee brace. Doc says I'm healing rather quickly."

"There they are," Glenda announces seeing Dillon guiding Mysti toward them.

Glenda, Devan and Danna all hug Mysti in welcome. She is also greeted by Kip, Dathan, Kiersten and Kayla

"We saved seats for both of you," Dathan informs as he directs Dillon and Mysti toward side-by-side seats between his parents and himself. Mysti ends up sitting between Glenda and Dillon with Dathan on Dillon's right.

As the first performance begins, Mysti tries to sneak a glance at Dillon who seemingly is sneaking a glance at her as well. An almost devilish gleam of a smile envelopes Dillon's face causing Mysti to look away quickly.

Everyone becomes entranced in the performances. Bridgit and Elton perform various ballroom dances together as well as in larger group numbers, as do Brooke and Elias. Eventually, it is Parker's turn to do his first-ever tap solo. He performs wonderfully. The grand finale includes every dancer and is the extravaganza the show title promised.

After the curtain calls, the crowd begins to disperse. Dillon senses Mysti seemingly eager to depart, once again placing his hand on the small of her back, he maneuvers her along with his family to where they are meeting up with the kids. Whispering near her ear again, "Running off now would disappoint the kids."

"You're right," Mysti concedes.

All the children come rushing out from backstage to greet their families. The commotion is nearly overwhelming.

"Why don't we save all our discussions for now. It will be easier to talk at the restaurant. Everyone knows where we're meeting?"

A round of affirmative responses ensues.

Mysti tries to get to the kids so she can congratulate them before they all leave. "Hey, you amazing dancers," she gets the attention of the kids, "You all dance so fantastic. Thank you for inviting me to watch you. I am so glad I got to see how great you all are and I am so honored I got to witness Parker's first solo."

The quintet of kids, express their gratitude for Mysti's kind words. After hugging each of them, Mysti straightens intending to say her goodbyes to the adults and depart.

"You're going to dinner with us, aren't you Mysti?" Bridgit asks loud enough for her parents to hear."

"No, Sweetie. I'm going to get going," Mysti responds.

"Of course, she's going with us," Devan states simultaneously.

Mysti looks at Devan about to excuse herself. "The kids want you to be a part of this. So, unless you have a hot date somewhere else, I can't think of a good excuse for you to disappoint the kids.

Elias chimes in, "Uncle Dillon's going with us, so how could she have a hot date somewhere else?"

Silence befalls the Lubbers family adults, joyous laughter envelopes the children. Mysti's eyes widen. As always Mysti is glad for her olive complexion, keeping the flush she feels creeping up her face indiscernible.

Dillon chokes back an amused chuckle.

"How right you are Elias. Out of the mouths of babes flows truth," Glenda states.

Looking down at the cherubic faces pleadingly looking at her, Mysti covers her mouth with both hands, breathes deeply before saying, "How could I say no to the five of you?"

Bridgit and Elton high five, Elias and Parker fist pump and Brooke throws her arms around Mysti's waist.

"That settles that," Kip announces. "However, since you have a track record of," Kip air quotes the next two words and winks, "*getting lost* when you're supposed to be following someone, I think someone should ride with you."

Bridgit and Elton offer to ride with Mysti.

"Mysti?"

"Yes, Elton."

"Don't you like Uncle Dillon? Our moms said you saved his life and you guys were stranded in a cabin and had to spend time together. Did being stuck with him make you not like him?"

Mysti pauses to choose her words carefully. "Yes, I saved your uncle. Yes, we were stranded together for over a week. We got to know each other a little during that time and I like everything I learned about your uncle. What makes you think I don't like him?"

"I don't know. It just seems sometimes like you don't even want to be near him."

"Other times you two look at each other like our moms and dads look at each other and they love each other. It's just kind of confusing," Bridgit adds.

"Confusing is exactly what it is. I like your uncle. I think he's a pretty great guy, but I'm not sure if I like him just because I feel a strong connection to him due to the circumstances of how we met and were trapped in the storm together or if I like him because I *like* him."

"How are you going to figure it out if you don't spend time with each other now that you aren't trapped together? I mean if you would go out on some real dates, like boyfriends and girlfriends do to get to know each other, then maybe you could figure out if you like each other that way or just as friends. That's what my mom said dating is for. To decide if you're better as friends or if you can love each other.

"My dad and Uncle Dillon are really close because they are triplets with Aunt Devan. Sometimes they kind of read each other's minds and my dad says he thinks Uncle Dillon *really* likes you, but that you're both scared. I can't think of anything to be scared of now. Uncle Dillon nearly died. I bet that was the scariest thing ever. Nothing else could be that scary and you two got through that together."

"You two sure are smart and mature for your age. Is that why you kids keep trying to get Uncle Dillon and I together?"

"Guilty as charged," Elton confirms.

They arrive at the designated restaurant. "Let's keep this conversation between us, OK? We're here to celebrate your amazing dance abilities not talk about your uncle and me."

"But..."

"I'll make you a deal. If you drop it for now, I'll *consider possibly* talking to your uncle about it and *maybe* seeing if he *might* want to *try one date* to get to know each other better. Deal?"

"Deal," they reply in unison.

"You're going to come to our choir concert on Wednesday night, right?" Bridgit asks Mysti as they meet up with everyone in the lobby.

Mysti glances around at the numerous sets of questioning eyes awaiting her reply. "What time does it start?"

"Seven PM," Brooke answers.

"I should be able to make that after work. Where is it?"

"Same place we had the dance extravaganza," Elias supplies.

"OK, then. I'll do my best to be there."

"You can be Uncle Dillon's date," Parker offers.

The adults laugh, the other children agree, "Yeah."

"Good idea."

Thankfully, the hostess appears at that moment to take them to their table.

Sunday morning arrives bright and cold. All the arrangements have been made for the *First Annual Tree Judging Crawl*. All four participants and four parent judges meet at Kiersten's condo.

The parents have decided to take this seriously and have arrived wielding clipboards with checklists of judging criteria and a point scoring system they'd devised to keep this fair.

"We decided that we needed guidelines for each of us to adhere to in order to ensure the fairest outcome," Glenda explains.

Kiersten ponders, "But there are, in a sense, two different competitions. How will they be able to differentiate if they don't know the teams?"

"We'll rank them one through four. Then the highest scoring in each of your two categories wins," Wally offers the solution.

It is agreed. They all enter Kiersten's place to find the first living tree to be decorated in a gorgeous palette of maroon, teal, turquoise, white and silver. Her strings of lights are soft white. It is a very classy designer look. The judges each make thorough, detailed inspections, jotting notes and scoring various aspects then totaling each judges score, adding them together then dividing by four to determine the average total score. The process and result are kept secret.

Kiersten has baked cider spiced, apple cupcakes with cider spiced coffee buttercream frosting. They are served with Hot spiced apple cider.

"We decided to each make a snack to serve to keep you fortified and as thanks for doing this for us," Kiersten informs.

The judges decide to add a separate food and beverage category to the competition. The crawl continues to Harlan's.

Kiersten and Harlan have decorated Harlan's tree very much traditionally. Very homey, in traditional multi-colored lights with the masculine touch of ornaments of old trucks, old cars, sleds, toboggans, skis, etc. The judging process is repeated. Harlan has prepared maple and brown sugar chewy blonde brownies served with hot Chai Tea Latte.

Next, they go see Dillon's tree, which Dillon and Harlan have decorated in various brown tones, russet, cream and gold with pops of deep red. The strings of lights are red and muted yellow illuminating scattered sprigs of tiny pinecones and small clusters of cream and tan pampas grass. Very masculine and gorgeous. As before the judges take to their clipboards. Dillon provides moist molasses, oatmeal, raisin cookies with a cinnamon blend coffee.

The final stop on the crawl is Mysti's house. She and Dillon have decorated her tree with blue and white lights, blue, white and silver ornaments. There are icicles, snowflakes, and snowballs. Mingled with miniature dream catchers, small plastic horses, deer, wolves, birds and other wildlife, pinecones, a smattering of fall colored leaves with the bright pop of color being clusters of red berries. Mysti serves ice blue colored peppermint cupcakes which she has added a filling of a chocolate peppermint patty to each and topped with white coffee buttercream frosting sprinkled with silver crystal sugar. These are served with peppermint Ghirardelli hot chocolate.

The scores are tallied, recounted and recalculated.

Kip announces, "Each tree is amazing. So amazing that even though we used a scoring system we feel is absolutely fair and tried very hard not to influence one another with our individual reactions or be biased by whose tree we were judging, it came down to a two-point difference between first and second places with two ties."

Cora explains, "The two trees tied for first are Mysti's icy blue winter wonderland and Harlan's masculine traditional. Dillon's and Kiersten's designer trees tied for second."

The four participants look to one another a bit perplexed. Kiersten states, "That means the two trees decorated by the 'couples' are tied for first and the two trees from the male vs. female challenge tied for second."

"As for the delectable treats and beverages?" Glenda informs, "Each pairing was so perfectly harmonic and appropriately coordinated with their corresponding tree it is impossible to choose one over any other. You all win."

Harlan concludes, "Spa Day for four and two home-cooked meals it is."

~ 7 ~

Mysti sees Dillon standing just outside the front door of the auditorium as she approaches. "Why are you standing in the cold?"

"Awaiting the arrival of my date," Dillon opens the door allowing Mysti to enter.

"About that. We need to talk sometime soon."

"Don't worry, Mysti. I'm merely humoring the children. There's no need to talk about it, I don't expect you to view this as an actual date."

"The children seem to be a bit determined on the matter of you and me. In an attempt to appease them, I kind of made a deal with Bridgit and Elton," Mysti informs somewhat sheepishly.

"What deal did you make?"

"I agreed to discuss with you the possibility of the two of us going on a *real* date."

Dillon's expression, from serious to smirk, was a slow glow that caused a glow of warmth to spread across Mysti's face.

Mysti rushes to explain, "Bridgit told me her mom explained that a date is a way for two people to get to know each other and figure out if they like each other as friends or if they like each other as boyfriend and girlfriend to possibly fall in love. The kids seem to think you, and I need to figure that out."

"I think they are correct. We do need to figure this..." Dillon gestures at the two of them, "...out. With all the activities going on with the holiday and our families seeming to meld together, I don't know when we can find time for the two of us to schedule a *real date*."

"We'll work it out at some point. There's no hurry."

"Hurry you two! You need to get seated before they begin," Kayla calls to them as she approaches. "We've got your seats saved. Come on."

Bridgit and Elias have solos in group songs plus the five of them perform a beautifully harmonized quintet of *Let There Be Peace.*

Mysti videos that piece to share with her family. She is amazed at how well these kids get along and work together, but also how disciplined and talented they are.

After the program, Mysti expresses her pleasure and congratulations then excuses herself, explaining she has to be up early for work and needs to get home to spend some time with the three bears before bed.

"You're bringing them up this weekend for the festival, aren't you?" Elton asks.

"Yes, of course. They always go up there with me and everywhere else I can take them as often as possible."

"Cool. Can we play in the snow with them again?" Elias asks.

"Sure. I'll be seeing you all in a few days. Goodnight."

Farewell hugs all around. Mysti turns to depart. "I'll walk you to your car," It is a statement, not an offer. Dillon walks beside Mysti, bringing smiles to the family faces behind them.

"About what we talked about earlier..." at Mysti's quizzical expression Dillon continues, "Scheduling a *real date*? I was wondering if maybe you and I could go for dinner Friday night? That way we can have a better grasp on where we stand before the big family weekend."

"Good idea. I guess Friday works as long as we don't stay out too late since we have to be up very early to head up to the festival."

"My car is fixed. I'll pick you up at six?"

"Sure. Six Friday it is. Where do you want to go?"

"It's a surprise. Dress nice," He winks.

"Don't I always?" Mysti feigns dismay at the imaginary accusation that she doesn't always dress nicely.

"Yes, you always look wonderful. I merely meant perhaps a bit dressier for this outing."

"Ok, then. See you Friday at six," they fumble between a hug and handshake in parting.

Midday Thursday, Hugh asks Mysti, "What's eating at you?"

"I was about to ask the same thing," Harlan joins.

"Nothing."

"That's a crock. You have been withdrawn all day," Hugh tells her.

"Sorry. I just have a lot on my mind with the holidays, getting ready for this weekend and this new project. That's all."

"Are you sure?"

"Yup."

"Ok, then. At least try to look up from your computer once in a while, so we don't have to only see the top of your head," Harlan encourages.

Early Friday morning Autumn catches Mysti looking at dresses online at her office desk.

"Spill," she commands.

Startled, Mysti goes to close the store tab on her computer, then realizes she could use her sister's help. "I made a deal with the Lubbers family kids that I'd go on one real date with their uncle so we could try to figure out if we like each other as just friends or as more. Dillon agreed. So, we are going to dinner tonight and he said to dress a bit dressier for where we are going. I realized this morning I don't have anything dressy. The only dress I own I wore in high school."

Autumn rubs her hands together rapidly in joyful fashion, a giddy expression upon her face. "Yay. Let's go shopping."

"We can't go right now, we're working."

"What good is it having your parents as your boss if you can't occasionally be spontaneous? Dad?" Autumn calls across the office. "I'm taking Mysti dress shopping." At her father's surprised look, she continues, "Mysti's going on a *real date* with Dillon tonight and she needs a dress."

Wally stands, withdrawing his wallet from his pocket as he crosses the office to hand his credit card to Autumn. "Enjoy your afternoon girls. Dress, shoes, accessories, hair... Do her upright," he tells Autumn.

Mysti's jaw-dropped expression receives a warm fatherly kiss on her cheek and tender smile.

Autumn grabs Mysti's hand practically hauling her from her chair and dragging her toward the door. "This is going to be fun!"

Autumn drives Mysti to a quaint dress boutique in Old Town where she has her try on a wide variety of dresses, finally settling on a bit fancier version of the typical little black dress. It is black lace with a jagged multi-length hemline overlaying a black silk sheath. It has a sweetheart neckline with a standup collar and elbow-length cuffed sleeves. They pair it with charcoal-toned nylons and fur-cuffed, thermal-lined, black high-heeled dressy ankle boots.

They also pick out a silver, front V, flat, serpentine necklace and silver dangle earrings.

"This is crazy. We're going way too overboard. This isn't some special romantic occasion. It's just a single date to appease his nieces and nephews. This way we can tell them we tried and we're better as just friends," Mysti tells her sister as they drive away from the boutique.

"I thought the idea was to determine *if* you're better as friends or more than friends."

"Technically, yes, but..."

"That's why we're going to do this right. Give you the total experience."

"Where are you going? Home's the other way."

"I know. I'm taking you somewhere else."

Autumn takes Mysti to get her long silky sable locks trimmed and coiffured. Mysti also receives a mani-pedi.

Autumn drives Mysti back to the office to pick up her vehicle then follows her home to help her finish getting ready.

"What time is he picking you up?"

"Six. What time is it now?"

"Five-forty. Wait here. I have to get something out of my car."

At the boutique, Autumn had spied a beautiful dark red, three-quarter length, long sleeved, split front, hooded, alpaca cloak with black faux fur trim. While Mysti had been in the dressing room, Autumn asked the clerk to ring it up and bag it. She'd then snuck it out to the trunk of her car without Mysti seeing it. She now brings it in and hands Mysti the bag.

"What's this?"

"A little something to keep my sister beautiful *and* warm."

Mysti opens the zippered garment bag to reveal the garment, "Oh, Autumn!" she exclaims. "This is absolutely gorgeous. You shouldn't have, but I love it."

"It feels like we're getting you ready for winter formal or prom."

"Since I never went to any school dances, I guess this is as close as I'll ever get, but it's just a dinner date."

"This is better than a school dance. You don't have a curfew and no parents waiting up for you," Autumn winks.

"Ha-ha. Very funny," with that, the doorbell rings. Mysti tenses.

"I'll get it. You calm yourself and come out when you're ready."

"Hey, Dillon. Wow, you sure look dashing. Come on in. Mysti will be out in a minute."

"Thanks," Dillon enters.

"So, where are you taking my sis to dinner?"

Dillon smiles. "It's a surprise."

"Aww, come on, you can tell me."

"She can tell you tomorrow."

Autumn sees Dillon's eyes widen, hears his sharp intake of air as Mysti obviously comes into view. Autumn turns to witness Mysti's entrance. Autumn's face beams with pride and joy at seeing her sister's full radiance as a coy smile creases Mysti's face.

"Wow! You look... Just wow! I can honestly say I have never in my life seen anyone more breathtakingly gorgeous."

Autumn's eyes fill with tears of joy that softly trickle down her cheeks at hearing those words spoken to her amazing sister.

Mysti lowers her gaze shyly. The glisten of moisture that springs to her eyes makes them sparkle, merely enhancing her beauty. She inhales a deep fortifying breath before venturing to fully face the devastatingly handsome man slowly moving toward her.

"You are very debonair this evening," Mysti utters, taking in Dillon's sleek black suit with black dress shirt and deep red tie.

Dillon halts but a foot before her. Their eyes meet. They both swallow firmly.

Autumn takes in the coordinated nearly matched outfits, "If I didn't know better, I'd think your outfits were preplanned. I guess great minds do think alike."

Realizing Mysti and Dillon barely acknowledge her comment, so lost are they in each other at that moment, "I think I'll be going now. You two have a great evening," Autumn announces quietly trying not to shatter the spell the other two seem bound in.

Mysti recovers first. "Autumn? Thank you so much for all your help today. Please drive home safely. I'll see you tomorrow up at the cabin. Oh, are you riding up with anyone or driving?"

"Mom and Glenda have the carpooling all figured out. We're all supposed to meet at the shop so we can leave extra cars locked in the yard."

"What time?" Dillon has come out of the spell of moments before.

"Our mom said eight, so we can get up there with plenty of time to participate," Autumn answers.

"Let me get a quick picture of you guys to commemorate this evening and for proof for the kids," Autumn directs them to stand close together side by side and snaps off a few pictures on her cell phone. "That's good.

"And Mysti? You're welcome. I am so glad to have had this day with you," she hugs her sis. "You two have an amazing evening and if you're not there by eight. Don't worry. We'll leave without you and the two of you can get there whenever," Autumn winks at Dillon and sticks her tongue out at her sister when Mysti graces her with a stern look.

After Autumn's departure Dillon gestures toward the door, "Shall we?"

Mysti picks up the gorgeous cape, which Dillon takes from her to assist in putting it on.

Dillon drives the twenty minutes to the restaurant where he booked a reservation. It is an old Victorian farmhouse renovated and added to, to become an upscale dining establishment. Mysti is pleased to find they have a variety of vegetarian entrees.

They order from the Dinner-for-Two menu, choosing the breaded baked artichoke heart appetizer with vegan garlic butter dipping sauce, mixed greens salad with Italian dressing, followed by the vegetarian lasagna made with house-made vegan mozzarella and finish with freshly baked fudgy brownies topped with house-made vegan, oat-milk vanilla bean ice cream and hot fudge.

Their discussion varies from work-related to family topics to the upcoming weekend adventure. As the meal winds down so does the conversation. There is a five-piece band consisting of piano, saxophone, standup bass, violin and drums, in the lounge area.

Dillon stands, offers Mysti his hand, "Will you dance with me?"

"I don't know how to dance."

"I promise, I won't pull any fancy ballroom dance moves on you," Dillon smiles encouragingly while also pointing to his still-braced knee.

Mysti smiles, accepts his hand and they walk to the dance floor to join a few other couples.

Once there, they begin to sway gently to the music. After a few moments, "I enjoyed the time we spent together in the cabin, however, this is by far much different, yet just as enjoyable."

"Yes," is all Mysti seems able to utter in response, as she feels cocooned in the pleasure of this moment, unlike any she has ever experienced.

Dillon allows her to remain drifting in the magic of the music and movement. The song concludes, they make their way back to the table.

"So, how do you think this experiment is going?" Dillon asks. At Mysti's perplexed expression he clarifies, "You know, the one the kids mandated of us going on a real date to see if we are better as just friends or more."

"Ah, yes, that experiment," Mysti now fully out of the mist of the dancing, "How do you think it's going?"

"I asked first," Dillon states in a teasing tone.

"Fine," is Mysti's monosyllabic response.

Dillon's brows draw together, "Fine, I asked first or as in the experiment is going fine?"

"Both?"

Dillon smiles, "Agreed." After a moment, "Mysti?" he continues once she looks at him, "Thank you. Thank you for tonight. I didn't think I was ready to trust again, but..." he pauses then asks a question that has taunted him for a while now, "I know we talked about your situation with James, but Autumn mentioned you have also gone through a heartbreak. I'm sure she was referring to James, especially since the night of his call at the cabin you called out in your sleep for Jeff," Mysti's intense inhalation and look of shock startles Dillon. "Mysti, I'm sorry. I didn't mean to upset you. I don't want to hurt you. I can't imagine how anyone could ever hurt you."

Mysti hears the sincerity in his voice, but she isn't ready to discuss this, not yet, not tonight. Tonight is going so well. She is struck by the realization she hasn't thought of Jeff even once tonight. Now she is upset for allowing herself to be distracted by Dillon's good looks, kindness and charm.

"I can't discuss that yet, not tonight, maybe soon."

Dillon decides to let it drop.

They take to the dance floor for a couple more songs before making their departure. The drive back to Mysti's house is made in companionable quiet, both enjoying the calm beauty of the gently falling flurries and the peacefulness of the barely illuminated landscape.

"Under normal circumstances, I wouldn't have to ask, I'd rush around to open your door before you could, but..." Dillon gestures at his leg, "Please wait?"

Mysti smiles, "OK, Peg-leg, I suppose I could try to be ladylike and wait for you to open my door for me." That simple use of the nickname she'd given him before she knew his name lets loose a wash of memories of the mere few weeks they have known one another. Had it really only been weeks?

As Dillon opens the car door, Mysti hears each of the three bears sound the alert that someone is on the property.

"Aw, the bears. Hi, boys." Dillon states softly in the snow-muffled quiet of the night.

"Would you like to come in and see them?"

"Yeah, sure. I'd like that."

Mysti lets the three bears in the house through the doggie door that leads in from their patio room after she instructs them to shake off the layers of snow.

Dillon sits on a kitchen chair and gives them all some attention. Mysti excuses herself to change, so she doesn't risk one of the boys accidentally damaging her new dress or nylons.

Mysti emerges in a tan sweat set and slippers. She pauses at the kitchen door stealthily observing Dillon with her dogs. They all seem to be members of a mutual-like society. That idea touches Mysti's soul and warms her heart. Kodiak catches sight of Mysti and rushes over to her encouraging her to join the *love-fest.* Mysti obliges, rustling her furry beasts, scratching their ears.

Dillon takes in Mysti's comfortable attire, shakes his head gently, a twinkle lights his eyes, "Just as beautiful casual as dressed to the nines," he clears his throat, "I should get going." He stands to leave. "I'll see all of you in the morning. Goodnight bears."

Mysti had let her hair down when she changed. Her hair now rests in bold waves about her shoulder. "Take good care of mistress, Sable Locks, tonight," Dillon instructs as he reaches up to gently run his fingers through a silky, sable, curled lock.

Mysti's expression takes on a dreamy mien, her head tilts ever so slightly toward his touch bringing a tenuous, tender smile to his features.

"Arf!" Grizzly makes known his desire to be fed, effectively bringing a halt to the mesmerizing moment.

"Yes, boys, Mommy is going to feed you. Not that you're starving, you had food on the patio."

Dillon moves to leave, "See you in the morning. I had a great time tonight."

"I did too. Thank you. See you in the morning."

Dillon leaves. Mysti stands staring at the closed door.

Dillon sits in his car in the driveway staring at the house, he puts the car in reverse and departs before he is tempted to go back in.

On his drive home, Dillon muses on how he misses what they had at the cabin. He misses climbing into the cold bed and ultimately finding themselves cuddled close for warmth, but was it only for physical warmth? Dillon admits in that moment that he feels drawn to Mysti, connected to her in a way he's not experienced before. Surely, he finds her physically attractive, but he also finds her mind and soul attractive. He likes everything about Mysti as a person and he knows without a doubt he can trust her implicitly with his life... and his heart.

Mysti muses aloud to the boys, "Is what I feel for Dillon just a bizarre residual of the connection brought about by the manner in which we met? Or am I falling for him because I find everything about him attractive? Not just physically, but his goodness. The way he is with the three of you. The way he is with his nieces and nephews, his siblings, parents and my family too." Mysti pauses when she realizes all three dogs sit before her staring at her with their heads tilted to one side as if to say *"Duh, Mom, you like him."*

She laughs, "Don't look at me like that. OK. I like him, but that doesn't mean the feeling is mutual."

Kodiak looks to Grizzly and Polar then in unison they all tilt their heads the opposite direction, yet again staring at her, their doggy eyes so expressive. She senses their disbelief at the absurdity of her doubt of Dillon's feelings for her. "OK, fine. So, our feelings are probably mutual, but I'm not sure I'm ready yet. I still feel I'd be being unfaithful to Jeff."

Kodiak stands, lets out one deep woof then nuzzles Mysti, licking her hand and pawing at her with his bear-sized paw. Kodiak was Jeff's favorite when they were all pups. It seems now, Kodiak is trying to tell Mysti something. Maybe that it's all right to move on? That Jeff would approve? Part of her knows that's true, but part of her still holds doubt, feels traitorous for still being here and having a life to keep living.

Suddenly she recalls an interview that she watched a number of years ago with a movie celebrity who had just lost his wife. In the interview, he was asked how he felt about having to go forward without his wife. He told the interviewer that he'd had a conversation with a background actress on a set one day. During the conversation, he'd discovered the young lady had lost a child. When he asked her how she kept going and seemed to still be able to find joy, the young lady had told him that she believed it was her responsibility to live life more fully in honor of her deceased son. She felt that those who pass would be angry with those still living if they wasted the lives they are still gifted to be experiencing, by moping around, saddened for those lost. She told him the living were to enjoy life doubly, for themselves and their lost loved ones. He had told his wife about the conversation before her passing and she had agreed, telling him to continue to enjoy life. He decided to do just that.

Fortified by the thinking and beliefs from this memory Mysti decides to honor Jeff by living fully for them both. By continuing to share her love with other deserving individuals. Dillon seems deserving of her love and his second chance at life.

Morning arrives all too early. Mysti loads her suitcase, dog food and other supplies into her suburban before calling the boys to join her. Once loaded and the house locked, they make the drive to the Van Strien construction yard.

Cora and Wally have arranged for Kip and Glenda to ride to the cabin with them as well as taking the rather large quantity of food to feed the small throng descending upon Meadow Creek. Devan and Tyce drive their own vehicle with their three children; Bridgit, Brooke and Parker and take a good portion of everyone's luggage in the rear of their new Suburban. Kiersten rides up with Dathan, Danna, Elton and Elias in their vehicle. Brad has cleared his schedule to enable him to attend the whole weekend event with everyone so, Dillon, Kayla and Jessie ride with him. Autumn, Harlan and Hugh ride up with Mysti and the three bears.

The five-vehicle caravan ascends the mountain. The roads are clear as they haven't had much snow the past few days, so they make good time, arriving just after the celebrations get underway.

It is decided to go straight to Solstice Festival to enjoy as many of the festivities as possible then go to the various cabins later to get settled in.

"Hello, Mysti," Constance Waldeck greets.

"Oh, hello, Mrs. Waldeck. Hello, Josiah," Mysti returns the greeting.

"Looks like you brought a small village of folks with ya," Josiah observes.

"Well, Sir, you did extend the invitation to their whole clan. So, they all came plus a couple of extras."

"I see that fine-looking young man you rescued is getting along much better. He sure is smitten with you," Constance observes.

"Now, Connie, donch'ya go thinkin' 'bout playing matchmaker. These two young'uns will do just fine without yer two-bit yenta services," Ole Josiah teases.

Mysti notices Josiah's use of the nickname for Mrs. Waldeck, signifying to her that just maybe the old coot and prim woman are finally getting closer to admitting their feelings for each other.

Josiah and Constance go about greeting, meeting and welcoming the whole clan.

It comes time for the snow fort building contest and snowball fight. Teams need to be determined.

"Family against family?" Dathan suggests.

"Those are pretty unbalanced unfair teams," Autumn observes.

"We can give you Brad and Jessie," Dillon offers.

"Still that's fourteen to eight," Brad supplies the math.

"However, Hugh and Harlan should each be considered two on account of their size. Besides, five of ours are little kids."

"Ok, so Harlan and Hugh are rather large, but that just makes them easier targets."

"We'll be on Mysti's team," Bridgit and Elton offer to help even the teams.

"Me too. Then the teams will be even. Eleven and eleven," Parker offers, proud he has counted it out by himself.

"Deal?" Mysti asks Dillon.

"Deal. Let the building begin."

"You do realize we are a construction family?" Mysti reminds the Lubbers' family as they set out to construct their forts.

Dathan's, Danna's and Devan's eye widen and jaws drop at that reminder. "What were we thinking?" Danna asks jovially.

"Just because they can build brick and stick doesn't mean they can build snow and ice. It's not the same." Dillon tries to encourage his family.

"Yeah. That's right. We've got this," Kip cheers on his family.

Hugh hears Dillon's encouraging words and decides to hurl a few more words of doubt, "You're forgetting that as a family, we've been participating in this event for thirty years. We are the reigning champs the last ten years running."

Laughter and cheering erupt from the Van Strien team.

Looks of dismay wash over the Lubbers' team. Glenda calls out to her family, "Don't give up before we've begun. Positive attitude is a job half done. We'll stick together until we have won!"

The Lubbers' team hoot and holler getting ready to get down to the task at hand... building a snow fort to withstand the onslaught of snowballs from the Van Strien team.

Josiah has the three bears join him on stage to observe the festivities and to keep them out of the fray of action. He's known them since they were pups and they mind him well.

The competition rules are given before the start of building. Josiah takes to the mic on stage. "Ya have thirty minutes to construct yer fort. At the end of thirty minutes, an air horn will sound commencin' the start of the snowball fight portion of the competition. That'll run fer twenty minutes or end when a fort is rendered destroyed by the opponents as determined by the sideline judges consistin' of ten townfolks, five men and five women, unrelated ta any participants. There are four battlefields consistin' of two opposin' teams each. The grand champions are determined after all four battles are complete. The team with the least damaged fort wins. Everyone understand the rules?"

All eight teams cheer and raise their hands to signal their readiness.

"Ready? Set? ...GO!" Josiah calls out loud and clear.

Yelling, cheering and instructions ring out from all directions as eight teams begin a flurry of activity.

At the Lubbers' fort Kip, Dathan and Dillon begin creating a front wall base. Tyce, Kayla, Kiersten and Danna haul snow to them to continue building with. Glenda supervises the snowball ammunition creation with Devan, Brooke and Elias.

On the Van Strien team, Harlan, Hugh, Wally and Mysti construct two walls in the shape of a V while Autumn, Brad and Jessie haul snow to them. Cora oversees the ammunition creation with Bridgit, Elton and Parker.

Dillon looks over to check his opponents' progress and sees their walls are already twice as high and twice as thick as any of the other seven teams participating. He turns to Tyce, "We need a whole lot more snow and fast."

Tyce looks over at the other forts, "Holy crap, they are fast. We got this," he rushes off and informs the ladies to kick it into high gear. They do.

"Hooooonk!" blasts the air horn.

Immediately snowballs begin to fly every which way. The usually quiet mountain air is overflowing with laughter, cheering, yelling, squealing as people hurl, and are hit with snowballs. The first couple minutes Hugh and Harlan stay low behind the safety of the strudy walls they built. The V shape reducing the surface mass available for easily accessible assault by the opposing team thus minimizing the amount of damage that can be inflicted.

Dillon notices the visual absence of the two giants and calls over, "What's the matter? Hugh and Harlan afraid to show themselves? Are they trying to hold up your weak fort?" Dillon taunts. "Letting the women and children take all the hits?"

Hugh and Harlan are finally ready for action. They stand, each holding huge boulder-sized snowballs they had been creating while hunkered down behind the wall. They each take two steps back with the blocks on their shoulders. Then in shotput form, they hurl their snow boulders at the Lubbers' fort. Both make direct hits, causing massive damage to the front wall.

Seeing the boulders flying through the air, the Lubbers all step back to avoid injury. They then rush forward to repair the damage using the additional snow they'd just be 'gifted' to thicken the wall while still continuing their assault.

Two more snow boulders are created and hurled just before the final air horn sounds. Again, both make direct hits, but there is no time for repairs as the horn signals the end of the competition. Everyone comes out from their forts laughing and joshing one another.

Kip observes, "Your fort walls look unscathed."

Everyone looks around at all eight forts and someone from one of the other teams calls out, "You sure you didn't mix cement with your snow?"

Another man calls out, "If ever there's an apocalypse and we need shelters built we're looking up your family of giants," Everyone laughs.

The judges have been walking around assessing the forts. They now approach Josiah on stage to inform him of their decision.

"The verdict is in," Josiah announces over the PA system.

"I wonder who the winners are?" Someone calls from the crowd, teasingly sarcastic. A smattering of chuckles resounds.

"The winners and still reigning champions for the eleventh year straight, the Van Strien Family. Now, Y'all remember how well constructed this fort is when you need home or business construction and call Van Strien Construction Company," Josiah plugs their business.

A round of good-natured comments such as "That explains it," "Aw, not fair, they're professionals," are uttered by other participants and spectators.

The Van Strien/Lubbers clan winds down a bit before deciding to make their way to the cabins to eat and settle in for the night.

"Our cabin is the closest and largest," Cora states after everyone is gathered near the parking area. "We should all go there and have a good meal before dispersing to settle for the night. We have divvied out the sleeping arrangements and we can go over them to see if they are suitable for everyone."

Everyone agrees to that plan and follow Cora and Wally's SUV to their cabin.

Everyone pitches in getting things inside. The ladies team up to make a meal for 22 while the guys haul in luggage and supplies. The kids help haul in firewood while Wally gets a roaring fire blazing in the massive fieldstone fireplace.

Forty minutes later everyone loads up their plates with comfort foods such as plain mac and cheese for the kids and macaroni and three cheese with broccoli for the adults, vegetable pasta salad, oven roasted mixed vegetables and cornbread muffins with butter and honey,

Once everyone has found a place to sit to eat, Cora explains her thoughts on sleeping arrangements. "Glenda and Kip can sleep here in the queen bed in the first guest room and I thought Elton and Elias could sleep on the bunks in there with them. Dathan and Danna can sleep on the pullout bed in the living room. Devan and Tyce in the second guest room on the queen bed with Bridgit and Brooke on the full-sized bottom bunk and Parker on the top bunk. Wally and I will have our room as, there is only one bed in there. I spoke with Brad earlier and he offered that he has a second bedroom with two sets of bunks and a pullout couch so I thought he could house himself, of course, and Kiersten, Kayla, Jessie and Autumn could share the room with the bunks. Huge and Harlan can flip for the pullout and the other can sleep on the floor in Brad's living room. That leaves only Mysti the dogs and Dillon. I figured since the five of them have already spent a week and a half in her cabin, they worked it out then, they can do the same way this weekend."

Glenda is the first to respond, "That all sounds perfect."

Everyone utters their agreement and the migration to sleeping quarters gets underway.

Harlan, Hugh, Kayla and Jessie take Wally's SUV to follow Brad to his place. Autumn and Kiersten ride with Brad. Once there they decide the twins, Kayla and Kiersten will share Brad's bed. Jessie will sleep on the pullout. Autumn chooses to sleep in the recliner leaving Hugh and Harlan on bottom bunks and Brad in a top bunk, so no one has to sleep on a floor.

Mysti takes Dillon and the dogs to her cabin to get settled in. Upon arriving Dillon gets the fire roaring while Mysti brings in their bags and more wood. The boys romp a while before coming in to settle for the night.

"A return to where it all began," Dillon sighs, looking around the small cabin. *Was it really only a little more than a month ago?*

Finally settled in front of the fire to wind down before heading to bed, without much prior intent, Mysti speaks softly in the relative quiet of the peaceful crackling fire, "Jeff passed away suddenly three years ago. We had been high school sweethearts. After graduation he'd gone off to college, I'd stayed here to take on a larger role in the family business. After he graduated college, he returned and we picked up pretty much where we had left off.

"I knew his proposal was imminent. We had been planning our future together for so long. He was on his way to pick me up to go out to dinner. The coroner's report determined that he was gone before the car crashed into the tree from a large undetected blood clot that suddenly broke loose."

Dillon sits very quietly listening, allowing Mysti to impart this information from a state of solemn reminiscence. When she stops speaking, he merely takes her hand in his, saying, "I am truly sorry. Thank you for sharing."

Dillon sees tears trickle down Mysti's cheeks. He stands, still holding her hand, he urges her to stand also. They walk to the bedroom, climb into bed wordlessly, then cuddle close. Dillon holding Mysti comfortingly as they drift off to a restful slumber together.

The sounds of dogs needing to be let out wakens Mysti and Dillon. Wrapping a fleece throw blanket around herself to ward off some of the chill morning air in the cabin, Mysti goes to let the dogs out.

Dillon hurries to the fireplace quickly rebuilding and restarting the blaze.

The duo falls into the ease of the morning routine of their previous adventure in this cabin.

Coffee made, breakfast cooked and eaten, turns taken in the bathroom, dogs fed, they are now ready to depart to meet up with everyone at the festival for day two activities.

The combined contingents converge upon the day two Solstice Festival events. Throughout the day various members participate at different crafting booths set up inside the large barn of the feed and grain store. They create Solstice themed gifts such as pinecone birdfeeders, birdseed filled milk cartons decorated with items collected from nature. They make garlands made of popcorn, cranberries, carrot slices, and various nuts. They skewer apples with carrots. These items are gifted to the wildlife that evening during the candlelight forest walk, which is illuminated by the nature decorated, stick mounted glass candle holders. The forest walk and feed disbursement are followed by the bonfire finale, complete with marshmallow roasting, smores and a cider and a hot chocolate bar. There is singing of solstice carols to say farewell to the old celestial solar year and welcome the rising of the new solar year.

Gratitude and farewells are expressed to Josiah and Mrs. Waldeck. The combined families leave the festival at seven-thirty to return to cabins to pack and load before heading down the mountain. Arrival and subsequent departure from the construction yard, once everyone has returned to their respective vehicles, takes place well after midnight making workday morning with little sleep mere hours away for all. However, the consensus is that the weekend's events were well worth it.

On the trips to and from Solstice weekend, Glenda, Kip, Cora and Wally have discussed the idea of Glenda and Kip reciprocating the Thanksgiving gathering by hosting everyone at their home on Christmas day. On Monday both mothers contact their children to get their feedback about the idea. All agree it is a great idea.

Mysti, Autumn, Kiersten, Kayla, Devan and Danna make arrangements to do some last-minute shopping together Wednesday for gifts and food supplies. The six of them are having such a great time together, helping to pick out gifts for each other's families, telling family stories and laughing. They stop for lunch at Francie's Freshly Fine Fare. While waiting for their meals a slight lull comes over the conversation. Mysti looks around the table thinking about how they came to be together here in this moment. In a soft, thoughtful tone, "You know, everyone has been treating me as the hero that saved Dillon, but truth be told, if not for Kodiak, Grizzly and Polar hearing Dillon, then making me follow them, I'd never have known he was out there. Kodiak acting as a warming blanket kept Dillon from freezing until I arrived. Without Grizzly and Polar I wouldn't have been able to pull the toboggan to the cabin with Dillon on it. The three bears are the true heroes."

The other five ladies listen and ponder Mysti's observation.

"Well, then, we need to do something special for them for Christmas," Devan states.

"Yeah! I know! We should treat them to a doggie spa day tomorrow so they will all be fresh and handsome for Christmas day," Kayla suggests.

"That's a great idea," Danna agrees, pulling out her phone she begins searching for local Doggie spas and makes a call to get availability and pricing. "What breeds are they? Let me ask."

"Polar is Husky/Samoyed, Grizzly, German shepherd/Rottweiler and Kodiak is a Caucasian Mountain dog."

The lady on the phone hears the breeds and asks, "What is a Caucasian Mountain dog?"

The five ladies giggle their responses, "Huge."

"Giant."

"Think monster truck."

"His name says it all, Kodiak, as in bear."

"OH! OK, then... This will be a first," she explains they require current shot records and muzzles if they are at all skittish or aggressive. The appointments are scheduled.

"It will be interesting to see the groomer's face when she sees the boys," Autumn comments.

"I'd pay to see that," Kiersten also comments.

"Ooo, I know. One of us needs to go with Mysti, go in first and video the groomers' reactions so we can all see it and share it with the rest of the family," Devan suggests.

"I'll go with you, Mysti, if that's OK with you," Kayla offers.

"Sure. That probably will be funny to see."

They finish up lunch and head their separate ways. "I'll meet you at the spa in the morning," Kayla tells Mysti as hugs and farewells are given.

"See you then."

Christmas eve morning arrives and each household comes alive with a flurry of food preparations for the Lubbers/Van Strien Christmas potluck buffet the next day.

"Hello, Dillon," Brad answers.

"Merry Christmas Eve."

"Merry Christmas Eve to you too. What's Up?"

"I'm baking.

"You, baking? Will it be edible?" Brad teases.

"Yes. I made these MOR cookies for the tree decorating contest and everyone said they are great so I decided to make a batch for the potluck tomorrow."

"Hold up. I have three questions out of that one sentence. First; more cookies?"

"Yes, M-O-R, Molasses Oatmeal Raisin."

"Second; tree decorating contest?"

"Yes, Mysti, Kiersten Harlan and I had a Christmas tree decorating contest. I'll tell you all about it later and show you pictures."

"OK. Third; Christmas potluck?"

"That's actually why I'm calling you. I know your family isn't around and you obviously didn't go to your sister's. What are your plans for tomorrow?"

"Planning to just be home doing pretty much nothing."

"That's what I thought. Your plans are changed."

"What do you mean?"

"I mean, you're coming to my parent's house for the day. We are breaking tradition this year and having a combined Lubbers/ Van Strien Christmas potluck buffet and you're joining us."

"I don't want to intrude on your families..."

"You won't be intruding. Besides, it's obvious to everyone that you and Autumn have taken a liking to each other. Come spend the holiday with her."

"Are you sure?"

"Positive."

"What should I bring?"

"You don't have to bring anything, but if you want to bring something go for it. Everyone is bringing whatever, whether it's baked goods, appetizers, main dish, snacks, you name it we'll probably have it there. Oh, and not that it's mandatory, but the Van Strien family are all vegetarian or vegan."

"Good to know. What time?"

"We'll probably all begin arriving around ten thirty. Any time after that is fine."

"Great, See you then. And Dillon?"

"Yes."

"Thank you very much for inviting me to join you."

"You're practically family... Hey, Brad?"

"Yes."

"You're my best friend. I trust and value your opinion. Do you think it's too soon to... I mean, am I crazy? Can I trust that what I'm feeling is real and not just some kind of PTS type reaction?"

"Dillon, I have known you for how many years now? One; no, I don't think it's a PTS reaction. Two; Love makes us all a bit crazy, so yes, you're probably crazy, but not crazy to tell Mysti how you feel. Three; no, it's not too soon. We all see how much you care for Mysti and how much she cares for you. You both seem to be holding back. Out of fear? Out of self-preservation? I don't know what it is, but the love the two of you so obviously have for one another is worth any risk. Otherwise, the risk you're taking is losing the best thing that has ever happened to you and probably to her too."

"Thank you, Brad. That's what I was hoping to hear. Tomorrow is going to be a big day. I'm glad you'll be there with me."

"I dang well better get to be best man," Brad states, assuming he has figured out his buddy's plan.

"But of course! See you tomorrow."

~ 8 ~

Mysti loads the crockpot of vegan frankfurters in her home-made sweet, spicy barbeque sauce. Then she loads a crockpot of her vegan version of Swedish meatballs in its vegan cream sauce made from oat heavy cream, oat butter, oat flour with nutmeg and other seasonings. She also brings a big bag of eggless flat noodles she'll prepare later to go with the meatless balls. She has also made a batch of the cupcakes she made for the Christmas Tree Crawl contest and has all the ingredients to make the matching hot chocolate.

The various family units begin to converge upon the premises of Kip and Glenda Lubbers at ten-forty-five Christmas morning. The home becomes awash with lively activity, soothing music and joy-filled voices and excited squeals of the children as they tell everyone of the gifts, they received from Santa Claus earlier that morning.

The air is saturated with the glorious smells of the wide variety of prepared foods and those still cooking, which blend with the scent of fresh pine from the living Christmas tree as all the food is put out on an array of tables set up to serve as the buffet.

By noon, twenty family members plus Brad swarm the home like busy bees. When the doorbell rings, Glenda goes to answer it.

The commotion of moments ago mutes as nearly everyone looks around trying to figure out who isn't already there that they would be expecting.

Opening the door, Glenda is heard saying, "You made it. Welcome. Come in. I am so glad you decided to come."

As Glenda ushers the newcomers into the living room, "It is an honor to be invited to be included in your families' holiday celebration," Mrs. Waldeck's voice is heard, followed by the unmistakable sound of Josiah.

"Well, I'll be. This here is some mighty fine digs ya've got. I surely appreciate yer inviting us to join ya."

Everyone has now gathered to welcome their mountain friends.

Mysti goes to the two elders, hugging them in welcome, saying, "I don't know who invited the two of you, but I am so very glad they did and I'm extremely ashamed I didn't."

"Don't ya fret none. Mrs. Lubbers here called the day after the festival and extended the gracious invitation. Wasn't sure at first, but after Connie and I talked it over we decided this was a whole lot better than what we've done the past many years."

"What have you been doing?" Bridgit inquires.

"Absolutely nothing. Sitting home like any other day. A few times, the two of us have sat together doing nothing jus' ta change things up a bit," he winks.

Elton pipes up before anyone else has a chance, "That ain't gonna happen ever again," he takes on Josiah's accent, "The two of ya are gonna celebrate every holiday from here on out right here with all of us. Welcome to the first annual Lubbers/Van Strien Christmas celebration."

A chorus of "Here, here." "That's right." "Absolutely," and various other confirmations ring out in agreement with what Elton says.

Elton whispers to Bridgit, correcting himself "Except it isn't really annual since it's only a one-time celebration."

"Close enough," is her lighthearted response.

The festivities get underway. Plates are filled to be eagerly emptied. Children play in the snow with the three bears. Clusters of adults, in migrative fashion, sit or stand chatting on a multitude of topics.

Late afternoon the children have had their fill of both playing in the snow and waiting to open gifts. Five exuberant youths bound in the back door.

"When do we get to open gifts?" Elias asks for them all.

Glenda responds, "Now, seems like a good time. Get out of your snow clothes, make restroom stops and wash up then calmly meet by the tree.

Glenda informs the adults to gather for gift opening too.

Brad seeks out Dillon, "Do you have a plan?"

"I'm going to wait until this evening after the gift exchange chaos settles."

"Does anyone else know?"

"No! Only you." Dillon inhales deeply, "What if she says no? Worse yet, what if she says yes simply because I put her on the spot in front of everyone and then recants later?"

"Calm down. Mysti's not going to say no and she will never say yes if she isn't sure."

"I hope you're right."

"I am."

Everyone finds places to sit, perch on a chair arm or stand nearby. Bridgit and Elton take on the task of doling out the presents. Hugh requests some large trash bags and takes the job of gathering the wrapping paper for recycling.

Midway through the gift opening, Parker calls out, "Hey, wait! This isn't fair."

Everyone looks at him. His parents dismayed by their son's claim of unfairness at such a giving time.

"Excuse me? Son that isn't an attitude of gratitude. Christmas isn't about fair and equal gift getting," Tyce informs, sounding stern.

"No, you don't understand. I mean it's not fair because we didn't know that Mr. Josiah and Mrs. Waldeck were going to be here, so nobody got them any gifts. Can I give them some of mine?" he asks. The tears rolling down his cheeks are immediately joined by tears rolling down the cheeks of 22 other beings, so touched by the child's loving heart.

Josiah recovers first, being the usually tough ole coot he is, he sniffs hard, then wipes the tears from his eyes, "Young man that is mighty kind of ya, but I'm sure Mrs. Waldeck here will agree wholeheartedly with me in sayin' that the two of us got *the* best gift of all given here today. The gift of everyone's love and kindness by welcoming us into this home and into your lives."

All five children put down whatever gift they are holding and go hug both Josiah and Mrs. Waldeck.

Mrs. Waldeck softly sobs, so overwhelmed by the expression of love they are receiving. She wipes her eyes with her hanky smiling sweetly.

Brooke loudly proclaims, "I want you two to be our new adopted grandpa and grandma."

The other children loudly agree.

"Mom, Dad, is that ok?" Bridgit asks.

Every adult in the room nods affirmatively as Devan and Tyce respond, "Absolutely."

"Can they be our adopted grandparents too?" Elias asks.

"Absolutely," Dathan and Danna respond.

Kodiak lets out one loud "Woof" followed by one each from Grizzly and Polar. "Yes, boys, they can be your grandparents too."

Everyone laughs heartily before resuming the gift opening.

A calm afterglow has come over all in attendance. The children quietly play with some of their new toys, the adults sit sipping hot cider, tea or coffee. Dillon and Mysti are sitting cuddled on the couch. Dillon looks to Brad and nods, receiving a responding smile.

Brad, who has spent much of today with Autumn now gets her attention and merely nods at Dillon and Mysti, raising his eyebrows smiling. Autumn's eyes widen in question. Brad nods yes.

Autumn catches the attention of her brothers, forefinger to lips she tilts her head toward the couple on the couch, each brother in turn in the same manner nonchalantly directing the attention of others that way. Soon all the adults, plus Bridgit and Elton who have caught on to the silent conversation, are causally keeping focused on the situation.

Dillon smirks as he realizes he and Mysti are now in the *spotlight*. Dillon disentangles himself from Mysti, stretching, he stands. He glances around the room glimpsing tender smiles of encouragement from the array of faces covertly watching him. Fortified by the positive energy being emitted from them, Dillon turns to face Mysti, still sitting on the couch. He becomes aware of numerous phones being casually picked up and readied for recording the event about to take place.

"Mysti?" Dillon whispers.

"Hmm?" She responds looking up at Dillon.

"I know we haven't known each other very long, but in these few short weeks, our families have become very close."

Mysti's brows draw together as she sits up straighter, glancing around the room, seeing all eyes on the two of them.

Dillon reaches and takes Mysti by the hand, he continues. "I know we both have had our share of heartache and failed relationships. I didn't think I was ready to trust again. Then I met you. Soon after our return from the mountain, it struck me; I literally can trust you with my life. I know it took a bit of..." he glances at the five children watching intently and smiles, "youthful prodding intervention to get us past the self-constructed walls that were blocking us from giving *us* a chance, but once we agreed to and went on the *real date*, my soul sang out that it had found its mate. You," Dillon draws Mysti to her feet to stand before him as he kneels on his right knee with his left leg outstretched to the side, before her.

Tears began spilling from Mysti's eyes, locked with Dillon's while he spoke. She quickly scans the room, taking in twenty-one smiling, encouraging faces, beaming with anticipation.

"Mysti," Dillon holds up a beautiful rose gold promise ring with a single heart-cut chocolate diamond. "Would you do me the honor of agreeing to be my girlfriend?"

A momentary expression of perplexion crosses Mysit's features and she once again glances at the others whose expressions mimic her own, as it seems everyone else also thought a different question was about to be asked.

Mysti looks back into Dillon's eyes, "Yes, Dillon. I will be your girlfriend."

Dillon moves to place the ring on Mysti's finger then halts.

"But Wait! There's more!" Dillon states mimicking the product-selling commercials. "Mysti Van Strien, would you also promise to one day be my wife?" Dillon's eyes are now brimming with unshed tears of anticipation and love.

Mysti inhales completely, filling her lungs, swallows to clear the lump from her throat, exhales and whispers, "Yes, Dillon Lubbers, I promise to one day be your wife."

A resounding roar of cheering fills the house to its brim.

"Now, this *is* the first *annual* Lubbers/Van Strien Christmas Celebration," Elton tells Bridgit. The cousins high-five, then join the hug fest taking place.

The <s>End</s> Beginning

ABOUT THE AUTHOR

A mother, grandmother and fur-baby parent, now in her silver-haired years, Remi is finally concentrating on achieving her lifelong dream and goal of being a successful, prolifically published author in various genres.

DEDICATION

To the Surman girls who, in our teen years, would say "Tell us a story about..." then tell me the characters, aka: their then current love interests, who they wanted to have me create a "meet, fall in love and live happily ever after" story about, for them.

Those sessions helped stoke the flames my burning desire to become an author of the happily ever after stories that only happen in what I call my Adult Fairy Tales.